THE OCEAN AT NIGHT
A NOVEL

Leigh —
I hope all of your ocean nights are filled with wonder!
XO

Lorna Hollifield

LORNA HOLLIFIELD

10/23/20

The Ocean at Night

Copyright © 2020 by Lorna Hollifield

Published by The Yellow Bird Press, 3425 Maybank Hwy, Suite A, Johns Island, SC 29455

All rights reserved. No portion of this book may be reproduced, stored in a retrieval system, or transmitted in any form or by any means--electronic, mechanical, photocopy, recording, or any other--except for brief quotations in printed reviews, without the prior written permission of the publisher.

ISBN: 978-1-7339449-3-9 (paperback)
ISBN: 978-1-7339449-4-6 (Ebook)

This is a work of fiction. Names, characters, businesses, places, events and incidents are either the products of the author's imagination or used in a fictitious manner. Any resemblance to actual persons, living or dead, or actual events is purely coincidental.

Cover Art: Olivia Seitz

Author Photo: Morgan Allen

"The Ocean" by Nathaniel Hawthorne, The Mariner's Library or Voyager's Companion (1833)

"Cry To Me" lyrics by Bert Russell © 1962 Downtown Music Publishing, Kobalt Music Publishing Ltd.

For my dear friend, Jamie High. Here's something for you to read by the ocean...God knows we've spent many hours there with our toes in the sand and will spend many more. Perhaps it was on one of those famous summer nights back at Ocean Lakes that seeds of this story were first planted. Thank you for a lifelong friendship, my fellow beach bum.

The ocean has its silent caves,
Deep, quiet, and alone;
Though there be fury on the waves,
Beneath them there is none.
The awful spirits of the deep
Holt their communion there;
And there are those for whom we weep,
The young, the bright, the fair.
Calmly the wearied seaman rest
Beneath their own blue sea
The ocean solitudes are blest,
For there is purity.
The earth has guilt, the earth has care,
Unquiet are its graves;
But peaceful sleep is ever there,
Beneath the dark blue waves.
"The Ocean" by Nathaniel Hawthorne

PROLOGUE
JULY 14, 2019

The sun set to their backs, over the wide marsh, but its fading glow turned the churning ocean in front of them into a rippling, clotheslined blanket of solid gold. Most people were packing up their tents and coolers for the day. Only a few stragglers lingered behind; an elderly couple walking hand in hand, a couple of kids begging for a few more seconds to finish their sandcastle, and a curly-haired girl panning for treasures with a strainer as the waves broke. The surf wasn't angry, but it was also far from calm. It was rushing the beach with purpose, taking it over, inch by inch, narrowing the availability of sand where they could take their evening walk. But Chloe didn't need too much room to run and squeal, just a strip of earth wide enough to accommodate her meager width plus a swinging sand bucket. Her tiny feet didn't take up a lot of space, and her footprints weren't all that much larger than the little four-taloned divots left behind by the prancing seagulls. Her blonde hair was curling at the roots a little bit, and it fell into piecey, saltwater-made locks at her little freshly tanned shoulders. Summer was all over her—her skin, her hair, her feet, and most of all, her spirit. Summer had always had a way of clinging to children like the dew would cling to the morning grass…a fact of nature, one of life's great partnerships.

The bucket full of sand, shells, and one small shark's tooth felt heavy around her little arm, but she managed, trudging on, her other hand embraced in someone else's. That's where she was first told of the legend, the one steeped up to the neck in the folklore mystery that she, herself, would become a part of soon enough. She didn't know that her freedom was set to a timer, a faulty hourglass, spilling out too quickly to plug up again. She was blissfully unaware that the setting sun was counting down the minutes, each purple or orange streak across the sky ushering her down a predestined path that she wouldn't choose to take, but was signed up for anyway.

They were just stories—the tales of the ones who went before her, based on truth, added to over the years—stories where a missing native tribe, an unfortunate shipwreck, and a crudely made cemetery collaborated to fashion an eerily-nicknamed sea island where people came only to vanish. It didn't matter that some of the events had happened hundreds of years apart, or that maybe far worse things had happened in other places around the famously haunted South. It only mattered that more than one mystery graced the same patch of sandy earth, and thus had created a reputation. It was that reputation that led to the additions, the ghosts, the warnings...Folly Beach, once known as *Coffin Island,* had the unique ability to make people disappear.

"I love the beach in the night time, don't you?" The adult beside the little girl spoke. "You know, Chloe, there's a spooky story about Folly Beach that goes way back, to like 400 years ago. Do you want to hear about it?"

Chloe nodded, more focused on skipping over the pieces of driftwood that were getting harder for her to see by the second than she was the person speaking to her.

"You sure? It might be a little scary for a girl your age." The palm trees rustled in the blackening distance, blending in with the sound of the crashing waves.

"I like scary stories. I'm not a little baby, you know." Chloe looked up and scrunched up her little freckled nose.

Her company paused for only a moment then began, "Well, there used to be a tribe of natives that lived here called the Bohicket. When the first white men came from all the way across the Atlantic Ocean, they lived everywhere around here, but in less than a hundred years they were all gone without a trace…they just disappeared, and none of the tribe could be found anywhere…not ever again."

"Are natives Indians? Like in Peter Pan?"

"Yes. Christopher Columbus only called them Indians because he thought he was in India, on the other side of the world. Native is a better word. It means they were born here. They were first."

"Oh…well, what happened to them? Why were they all gone in a hundred years?" She bent down to fiddle with a spiral shell.

"It's assumed that they all died, but nobody really knows why…if it was sickness, or war, or buccaneering pirates, or what."

"Pirates aren't even real. They're just monsters. *Pretend.*" Chloe stood up and shook her head, putting her free hand on her hip.

"Pirates were monsters, but very real ones. They didn't come from Neverland or have hooks for hands, but they were boat robbers. There was a terrible one called Blackbeard who spent time in these parts, taking anything he wanted…from the white men, the natives, or whoever else he saw out on the water. I think most of the Indians were gone by the time he came through though…except maybe for their ghosts. Those might still be here, around us right now. I've heard that in the evenings they still walk right out of the sea oats and onto the beach, never truly leaving their home."

"Ooh, creepy," Chloe giggled nervously as if she were on a haunted Disney World ride, *almost* loving every second of the thrill.

"But that's not the only time a whole group of people disappeared on this beach. In 1832, almost 200 years later, a ship called the Amelia that was headed for New Orleans, Louisiana wrecked right here. The passengers fought their ways to the shore, thinking they had survived it…but instead they were quarantined and left all on their own out here."

"What's quar-an-tee?" Chloe eked out, and quickly looked toward the dunes to check for ghost Indians.

"*Quarantined*. It means shut off, kept where they were, trapped."

"*Why?*" Chloe stopped in her tracks and looked the storyteller in the eyes, her own now enormous with awe.

"There was a rumor that the passengers from the boat might have Cholera, which made people very, *very* sick, and could wipe out entire towns within months. The locals didn't want to spread it, so they just left the passengers from the Amelia to fend for themselves on the little empty island. They didn't have food, or houses, or anything. They had to make shelters out of driftwood and palm leaves and ride out the stormy, wet nights. Many of them died right here on this beach that we're standing on, trying their best to survive."

"So is that why they call it...what did you tell me...Coffet, Coffee..."

"Coffin Island?"

"Yeah, *Coffin* Island. Is it because so many people died here? Isn't a coffin that thing they put you in before they bury you down in the ground? Like when my Grandpa Bill went up to Heaven?"

"Yep, sure is. You're such a smart little girl, Miss Chloe."

"I know." She shrugged.

"So a lot of people ended up in *their* coffins right here on this little stretch. Even long after the natives died out and the shipwreck happened, this place was used as a burial ground for Civil War soldiers too. But, I guess you're still a little bit too young to know much about the Civil War just yet." The grown-up paused, "The point is, it just seemed that people came here to disappear, or at least to become invisible, because once they got here, nobody ever saw or heard from them ever again."

"*Scary.*" Chloe added, kicking at the thicker sand near the dunes where the beach exit was.

"Some of it…most of it maybe. But also, intriguing. Part of me thinks it's nice that there's a place on Earth where you can go to and just blend in with the other tourists, fade into the moonlight, and forget who you were somewhere else in some other time and place. You know, Miss Chloe?"

"What are you even *talking* about now?" She looked up, her two missing bottom teeth showing when she sniggered.

"Nothing."

"Are we invisible when we're here? Did we come to disappear like a magic show…like those Bo—Bo—Bohickeys?" She twirled about, giggling whimsically with the strengthening breeze.

"Yeah, I think we did, Miss Chloe…I think we did."

PART 1

TEAL

CHAPTER 1

"Mama and Uncle Hank are wrestlin' in the bedroom again. It's real loud this time. I can't sleep, Teal." Huck trotted into my bedroom, which was a whole kitchen and living room away from his and Mama's rooms on the other end of our little *almost* house.

I called our place an "almost house" because it wasn't quite a whole one. It was more like whatever was left of what used to be some rich guy's weekend place in the sixties. The tin roof seemed cute to the tourists that came out to Folly Beach every season, down from the mountains or Ohio (I don't know why so damn many from Ohio), but it was loud in a storm and attracted the lightning too. Our place was struck two different times, and once so bad that the fire department had to come out, and we ended up having to stay in a motel for two whole weeks. On top of that, the white paint was coming off the old Gullah-built stone siding, and the windows had already been rusted shut for years, although one of the famous Charleston-green shutters did cling on till the very end. Stubborn little bastard. It was the one outside of the window above the kitchen sink, a place where most people probably remembered their mothers standing to clean up after dinner. That's not how I remember my mother, though. That sink didn't see much action; nor did the stove or fridge, for that matter. But that *one,* that mule of a shutter, was the ruler of the kitchen, hanging on through wind, hurricanes, rain, and failing hardware year after year. A true Folly Beach, South Carolina native to the core. I kind of respected that old piece of half-faded wood. It didn't choose to be a part of that broken down place, but it sure held its ground, rooted in deep like a century-old live oak.

As for everything else that was falling apart around there, it just had to be. Mama refused to ask the landlord to do a thing about any of it. I assumed it was because he was also her boss, and she didn't want to rock a boat that wasn't all that steady to begin with. But Ol' Limeberry...he was everybody's boss. He was probably used to keeping people up. Even "Uncle Hank" did odd jobs and handy work for him when he wasn't too drunk for it. One would think *he* could have fixed some stuff for Mama from time to time, but Uncle Hank wasn't much for doing people favors. He only did enough on the job for Mr. Limeberry to make sure he signed his name to the bottom of the paychecks. Mr. Limeberry signed the bottoms of all of our paychecks. It seemed like he owned three quarters of the houses on Folly Beach, not to mention the rest of the South Carolina coast. He had two or three restaurants, a laundromat and an ice cream shop too. He was the fat cat with expensive boat shoes and too much waist for his salmon-colored golf shorts…just like all of them were with two nickels to rub together—the *other* half of Folly—not the half that I was any part of.

Mama handled the weekly rentals, but a lot of times, I did. We rented the houses out to tourists for Limeberry Properties. It was mostly vacationers, but occasionally we'd get an artist or a writer hiding away, trying to suck some inspiration out of the salt water. Everyone seemed to believe that they would somehow be able to strain all the majesty out of the ocean like curd through cheesecloth, and *sometimes* it seemed that they could manage to do it. If they believed it enough they could. Never a born-and-bred though. Maybe we were just too close to the magic all of the time, and the exposure had cursed us more than it had cured us. I'm a firm believer that there absolutely *can* be too much of a good thing. The ocean without moderation is liable to drown a person fast. It sweeps them up in the tide either because they can't get enough of it, or because they've already had too much of it and just can't keep kicking any longer. Point is, when you live by the water, sometime or another, you'll find yourself in over your head. The tourists would come for just a little taste, and it'd last them all year. Me...I loved the water as much as anyone ever could; it was in my bones as much as the marrow itself. But at the same time, my legs were getting weak from all the years of treading.

My favorite vacationers were the ones riding in solo, showing up with a face so broken it might as well have been whacked with a Louisville slugger. Those were the ones I'd see out walking on the shoreline after the sun had gone down, using the glow of the moon to try and find whatever part of themselves they'd lost somewhere in a big land-locked city, knowing damn well they weren't apt to find it out there either. But I got it—a person still had to look. Three quarters of the earth is ocean water, so the math lied to us, told us whatever "it" was that we wanted was sooner or later going to wash up on that beach. So we hoped by the odds of it, that it would, even if it just came in the form of some hairbrained revelation spewed out from something that we felt small when standing next to. I think we've all had the need to find something in nature that's felt like home and ask it for some guidance.

So I always understood the broken kind the most. They felt like real neighbors, cut from the same half-spoiled dough that I was. They wanted to be by the water, that was always the most stirred up under the moonlight, just to feel something...even if it was rage and frustration...or to look for a miracle that wasn't ever going to come. We were the ones that were always a little like the ocean itself. We were full of all that incredible energy that moved around all of the time but could never seem to stretch past the shoreline, no matter how hard it reached for it. Even if each time was a little further than the shot before, eventually it just wouldn't be enough. We'd have no choice but to pull back and try again next time in a new tide.

Now, I'd never speak to any of them, the ones like me; they wouldn't have liked it too much. When we'd spot one another though, we'd exchange a little look and recognize our own kind, two animals of the same strength. We'd keep a healthy distance like two lions passing one another by out on the open savanna, and we'd tip our sea-sprayed hats.

The ones like me were few and far between. It was mostly the happier people who sunbathed during the daylight hours that were our temporary neighbors. They'd show up during the holidays or the warmer months with surfboards that had never been ridden, and SPF 9,000. They'd ask where the best local seafood was, then go to a Bubba Gump's anyway, making us all swallow our vomit when they showed back up with the to-go boxes. I hoped they'd enjoyed that pre-packaged shrimp that was probably frozen a thousand miles away and half a year before they tried to digest it.

Anyway, we'd get the place clean enough for them, fix what we could, and then call Hank Feller for the rest of it. I supposed that's how he and Mama got together to begin with, working for Limeberry. But it wasn't the worst gig out there. In exchange, we got our own little shack that wasn't so cute when you were a year-rounder in a never ending battle with wind and water. Spoiler alert: the forces of nature always won that war. I spent more time cleaning sand out of my skivvies, and replacing storm door screens than I did anything else. Most of the work fell on me too. And the more beautiful and sunny the April to October season was, the more work I had to do. I was never the teenage girl throwing bonfires on the shore, or living in a bikini all summer long, though I admit when I saw them around, hanging off the backs of tricked-out golf carts with rims better than the ones on Mama's old Honda, I wondered what it might be like. I'd stop and stare at the smiling faces, and freckled shoulders for a minute, and wonder what their lives would feel like inside of my skin. I'd see the surfer boy in Ray-bans and board shorts, and wonder what it would be like to know him…even if he turned out to be dumb as a box of hammers (which I was sure he would). I'd wonder. Maybe he'd even think I was cute if I'd wipe the scowl off my face long enough. I'd been whistled at enough times to know they'd liked my natural blonde hair, and bronzy skin. I didn't have shabby features…just a shabby house. I'd think about it, for a second here and there…then pick up my tool box and go back to cleaning gutters and switching out rusty old locks.

No, I wasn't the girl squealing like a hog from the teenage caravan. And high school was over. I'd be eighteen by fall of the year. I'd missed my chance at the glory days. Instead, I was the girl that cleaned up the empty carnival grounds after they'd already packed up all the rides. I sifted through what was left of everybody else's fun…and it was really a terrible, eerie thing at times. I grew up as the undertaker of sunshine and summer nights. But it paid for fried baloney sandwiches and half the power bill just fine.

I had to do what I could to help. Mama had too much other stuff on her mind—like keeping a man entertained—to run the house in any sort of way. Those last couple months at the end of my fateful seventeenth summer, before Will Cianciola showed up and divided everything in my life into *before* and *after* him, it had been "Uncle Hank."

Mama used "Uncle" Hank's full name every time she addressed him. I guess she wouldn't have done it this way if his last name hadn't been Feller, which, of course, is redneck for *fellow*. So she'd always run around yellin', "Get your snow white ass over here, Hank Feller," or "Where's that Hank Feller gone off to today?" Or my personal favorite, "I can't get that pukin', drunk-ass Hank Feller up off my couch."

Mama had gotten me into calling him Hank Feller all the time, but to Huck, he was just good ol' "Uncle Hank," for that moment anyway. I used to think they really were my uncles when I was little like Huck. But then one of those "uncles" made Huck and took off before he could cry for the first time. I figured no uncle of mine would do such a thing, or that maybe "uncle" just meant something a whole lot different than what I thought it did. I was about ten when I figured that one out, so I figured Huck, at seven, had a little ways to go yet. He'd already been through a slew of faux uncles though, and I knew he'd learn, too, soon enough. No need to rush it. Turned out the word uncle could actually mean many things, some of them all right…and some of them uglier than slime on the very bottom barnacle of the pier that only showed its face at low tide.

I learned to tune them out, Mama and Hank Feller, tune them out, or put my earphones in. I'd shut out the screaming, or the yelling, or the loud, classless, um, *fornicating*? But I was also lucky to have the room on the opposite side of the house. I felt bad for Huck. Those walls were awful thin, and he was too young to learn the facts of life just yet. Especially with those two teachers. It'd been better to go down to a farm and watch the animals mate.

"Come on in, Buddy." I waved him in like I did anytime he trotted by my door with that look on his face. I tossed my half-shot second-hand earbuds to the side. "You can crash in here tonight if you want to, Huckie."

"But your room is so far away from Mama. I might have a bad dream and get scared." He pulled at a thread on the sleeve of his faded Mickey Mouse pajamas, nervously making a tiny hole an even bigger one.

"Well, I'll be here. I've dealt with a bad dream or two in my lifetime. I think I can handle it." I put my skinny tanned arm around his tiny shoulders, noticing how unruly his blond head had gotten over the years…so much like mine, and our mother's. You could spot a McHone from a hundred yards out just by the curly mess of gold perched on top of our heads.

"You're never here. You'll leave to go down to

the beach in the middle of the night lookin' for teeth for that tan lady you want to work for. You always do. I hear the screen door squeakin' when you sneak out there." He crossed his tiny arms and lowered his bed head.

"Not tonight." I shook my head. "The place is *still* crawlin' with cops. I went all the way up to the Washout tryin' to find some good shark's teeth. They were patrollin' even all the way up there and in the marshes too. They're still lookin' for that little girl that went missin' a couple of weeks back. They're out there all day *and* all night. All my little hidin' spots too. I don't know where I'm gonna have to go to find my next crop, and I'm due some to Ms. Garvin. She was nice enough to let me work with her a little bit, but I've got to come through on my end somehow. I want this new job to work out so I can get quit Limeberry before I'm Mama's age. I don't want to get stuck…" I trailed off, and could feel my eyes searching for something that didn't even exist yet.

Huck scrunched his nose up and asked a question that let me know he'd only heard half of what I'd said. "A little girl? Did she get snatched? Mama always tells me if I wander too far off from her that some bad guy will snatch me. Is that what she did? Get too far away from her Mama or Daddy?"

"I don't know. Hope not." I sighed.

"Will I get snatched too? Are the bad guys still here at our beach?" He eased off the doorway and scurried up onto my bed.

"She wasn't from around here. I bet she got in the water and didn't know how to swim or somethin'. Probably didn't know how to get out the undertow. She was little. Don't worry, Huck. Nobody's gonna hurt you. Plus, I'm not movin' a muscle tonight." I searched his worried face. "You're all right. I guess I shouldn't have said anything. I forget what a little guy you still are sometimes." I slipped my hand around him and pulled him into the crook of my arm before I whispered, "It's because we're besties."

"Maybe she didn't get lost in the water either." Huck said drowsily, snuggling in closer to me, "maybe she's just lost a little bit, like when one shoe is under the bed."

"Maybe so, buddy." I humored him. "I hope."

"Maybe the nice lady found her."

"What nice lady?" I bent around to look at him, making a double-chin for myself.

"The one at the beach." He yawned, trailing off, "I wanted to go to day camp with her. She said there were other kids, but Mommy wouldn't let me…said it'd prolly cost too much money."

I didn't think much of what he mumbled on about for a minute or two. I just tried to smooth his angry little curls while he shut his heavy eyes. But then I got to wondering, and asked, "Who are you talkin' about Huckie? What camp?" I scrunched my nose up. "Huck?"

But he didn't answer me. His chest moved up and down deeper and deeper, his breath filling his whole little pot belly before he let it back out again. So I rolled over, careful not to wake him and yanked the yellowing lamp cord out of the wall. Then I turned onto my favorite side and curled my skinny knees in toward my body. I let my own breath get longer and slowly take more time to clear out of my lungs, until the rhythm of it was even with Huck's. And I was almost there...almost to that sweet spot where the real world always changed to dreams when something popped into my head and sobered me back to life again.

It was the woman on the beach from the week before last...the woman I'd never seen before that night. She'd made eye contact with me, perfect eye contact, her hazel green to my blue...then she rushed away down the beach. I thought she looked wide-eyed and hurried, a strange thing to be on the lazy lowcountry beachfront in late July. I didn't even think about it then...the little girl she had by the wrist, I had assumed was her little girl. She kind of dragged her along as she whimpered. But whatever Huck had been mumbling on about, for some reason, made me remember her clear as day…and that memory dropped a rock that sank quickly down into the bottom of my stomach. It started out like a little pebble that night, but soon enough let me know, it had moved in for good, and was going to keep on growing every day. By the end of that summer, it would fill me completely.

CHAPTER 2

The house at the end of our block was the leasing office. It was kind of like the mullets I'd seen at the bad gas stations on the outskirts of town—neat as a pin up front where a pristine water cooler full of fancy cut-up cucumbers welcomed guests, but a disaster in the back with all the paperwork piled up on the false-wood desks. I supposed the sliced up pieces of unpeeled melon in the tap water were meant to impress, but personally, I'd rather just have had a Dasani myself. But to each their own.

It wasn't so bad spending my days there, but it wasn't so good either. I guessed that's how a lot of people lived, somewhere in the boring-ass middle, enough happiness to keep them from jumping off the end of the pier, with the assumption that life is just *like that*. Always half full. It didn't occur to me to hate my life, but I also wanted out of it.

Even so, I found my little bits of joy around the office, too. For instance, the whole place smelled like window air conditioners, the old school kind that dripped water down into a pie pan on the floor. And I loved the smell of window air conditioners. That smell was my little slice of melon in the sink water.

"Teal, get out here. I need to talk to ya for a minute." Mama shouted from the front desk, unknowingly striking the match that would light the fire that would change my life. Weird what a small, tiny bit of a moment it was at the time. I rolled my eyes (their color matched my name to a T) and stumbled around the corner with one leg trying to wake up from where I'd been sitting on it for half the morning.

"Whatcha ne—" I stopped speaking when I saw the tall police officer standing with his feet sprawled too far apart in front of me. Then I took note of the two other men—Mr. Limeberry, and *him*, the man the news had told me was Will Cianciola—that missing girl's daddy.

It was kind of like seeing a celebrity out somewhere. I mean, I'd not seen many of them, growing up in a tiny corner of South Carolina. Everyone in Charleston County had seen Bill Murray out and about somewhere, crashing private parties or playing bartender, or seen Darius Rucker, although Darius was usually trying his best to keep to himself. The thing with celebrities was, you felt like you knew them. You'd seen them around so much, on t.v., or Instagram, or in magazines, that you'd forget they weren't just any old neighbor you'd throw your hand up at when taking out the garbage. They had these familiar faces I'd gone to sleep looking at. It was the same way with Will Cianciola. He'd been everywhere the past couple of weeks. I'd flat out forgotten he was a stranger for a second, just standing there with my jaw on the ground like I was. But when I remembered myself after way too many seconds, I still tried to do him the courtesy of pretending it was a brand new introduction. He shouldn't have been famous around Folly Beach, and it was a sad reason why he'd become it so quickly.

"Teal, do you remember Officer Smathers, here?" Mama began. "You know, we went to high school together...I'm sure I've introduced you two at the Piggly Wiggly or somewhere over the years."

"Yeah, Tracy and I go way back." He winked at me awkwardly, his Folly Beach Police badge beaming off the sun that squeezed through the dingy blinds. "And I've seen ya around here and there. I don't think we've spoken since you were in pigtails though."

I smiled awkwardly, feeling five years old again,

sure the freckles on my nose were glowing.

My mother continued. "And the gentlemen standin' next him is Mr. Cianciola." She tried to sound so proper as she tucked her black bra strap back underneath her white sleeveless "office" blouse. It was nicer than her other shirts that always showed a touch of her stretch-marked midriff. She expected me to respond but instead ended up in an awkward pause while she searched my shocked face.

I could still feel my own mouth hanging as open as a screen door in a late April thunderstorm. I wasn't sure if I was only shocked, or maybe kind of afraid too. It was probably some of both, mixed up into some new thing I couldn't recognize. What did they want with me? I'd only been on the beach for a little while that night. I'd been hunting shark's teeth at low tide for Casey Garvin, the owner of Foxy Fossils. She made fine jewelry out of teeth, shells and even skeletons by dipping them into gold, painting them or encrusting them with jewels. I was determined to become her apprentice, to make something good out of the graveyard. All a beach is, really, is a big cemetery we morbidly like to collect from. I found something kindly romantic about it in a twisted way; but it didn't matter the reason. If I could pick up the trade, I could stop sitting on the sidelines of fun my whole life. Maybe I could get some famous Instagram model to pick up my designs and make me somebody. I almost lost myself thinking about it when I realized I was zeroed in on Mr. Cianciola's sunken-in face. Then my mind time-warped back to *that* night...the night the girl went missing.

I'd been distracted. I didn't even know if the little girl I saw *was* the right one. I just saw a girl and her mama. Of course it was her mama, the right age, the right look. Blonde-ish, like the little girl. That's it. A little girl pitching a fit on her mama for making her leave the beach. I'd have had no reason to think anything different. I hadn't seen a damn thing. I had no information about that disappearance for anybody. If I said something it would look as if I were just trying to involve myself to feel important.

The officer, who seemed to know me better than I did him, changed his demeanor all of the sudden and addressed me like it was business. "Miss McHone—"

"Teal is fine," I answered quickly, my mouth finally returning to its normal position.

"Teal, then, I'm part of the team workin' on Mr. Cianciola's case." He motioned to the even taller man next to him. "I'm sure you're aware of Mr. Cianciola's, er, *situation* by now."

"Not...not really." I began slowly *lying.*

The officer took a brief breath in, and let it out. "Mr. Cianciola is a general contractor, and has been doin' some work for Mr. Limeberry, here. He has been workin' on some of the residential properties in development and also vacationin' in the area since the fourth. Unfortunately, his six-year-old daughter went missin' in recent weeks. I'm surprised you haven't noticed the search efforts. Our squads have been all up and down the beach, and everywhere else for that matter. It's been around the clock."

"I—I've been workin' so much lately…just been in my own little world, I guess." I stumbled. "I—I collect fossils too. I make stuff…it's not important." I tried with a half grin.

His face didn't move, and I knew he thought I was an idiot. "So, ya haven't noticed anythin' out of the ordinary? Haven't seen anythin' out on the beach?"

I swallowed hard and shook my head.

"Well, our efforts haven't turned up what we might have hoped they would have just yet. While we investigate Chloe Cianciola's disappearance, her father will need to remain in the Lowcountry. Mr. Limeberry, here, was kind enough to reach out to us about donating room and board durin' the duration of the investigation."

Mr. Limeberry forced a humble smile, close mouthed, eyelashes angled at the ground. It was the same smile he had when he donated a hundred grand to the Medical University of South Carolina. I waitressed the event. I half expected someone to pop out from behind the panel of brochures about parasailing with a baby for him to kiss. He always loved being the community hero when one was needed, which always reminded me that I was still just the help.

"Well, I do feel just terrible about all of this. I feel a sense of responsibility for my little community. And, after all, Will was here doing work for me to begin with." Mr. Limeberry paused and rolled his lips into a sorrow-filled, what-a-damn-shame line. "So, I've arranged for Mr. Cianciola to stay in the cottage across the street from your house, Teal." He unrolled the lips and addressed me with a tone like a proud principal would to a reformed school bully, nice enough, but like he was owed a special favor for all he'd done for me. "And since the season is slowing down with school starting up again, I thought you might have some extra time on your hands to see to anything he might need—fresh linens, tidying up—acting as a concierge, of sorts. Your mother can run things here at the office just fine on her own, need be. And since you'll just be across the way..." He trailed off and smoothed his gray comb-over that I don't think he knew was a comb-over.

"Um...yes, of course. I, uh, anything I can do to help out."

"I appreciate that," the broken man said quietly in an accent I recognized but couldn't place, still gazing down at his leather flip flops.

"You're welcome, Mr. Ci—" I struggled with the name, "Ci-anc-i-ola. Sorry, that's not really a common name around here."

"Will," He looked up, the sadness shooting out from his dark brown eyes, and somehow winding up all over me. "I'm from up north. Lots of Italian names there. Will works fine, though."

"Will." I repeated quietly while he held my gaze.

Officer Smathers spoke again. "We'll keep security pretty tight around here. We should have officers patrollin' the area around the clock. You'll also see a lot of us around, due to the investigation. Please keep your eyes peeled for anythin' unusual. If you see somethin', even if you think it's nothin', tell somebody about it. Okay?"

I nodded, never able to work up a blink.

"I've got flyers with information and pictures of the girl now, Teal." Mama's chipped red nails fumbled through the stack of papers before she handed me half of them. "You can help pass them out here around town after you get Mr. Cianciola settled in over at the cottage."

"Thanks, Tracy." Officer Smathers nodded at her.

I slowly looked down at the stack that now rested

in my skinny, chewed-to-the-nailbed hands. She was adorable—a kindly crooked smile, blond hair and bangs, her father's puppy dog eyes. Then there were the facts, listed underneath her so coldly, just like a grocery list or something.

Chloe Paige Cianciola
Age: 6 years old
Sex: Female
Race: White
Hair: Blond
Eyes: Brown
Height: 3'10 (46 inches)
Weight: 43 pounds

Last seen: July 14, 2019 on Folly Beach, SC wearing light-colored jean shorts, a white tank-top with pink flowers over a pink swimsuit. Was carrying a red sand bucket.

I studied the paper. Was it the little girl on the beach that night? It sure as hell looked like it, but didn't all the little girls look something like that? Little bangs, lighter hair than they'll have as grown-ups? Couldn't I have seen some other little girl? I couldn't remember what the child had been wearing. I knew I hadn't seen any sand buckets. And I knew I didn't want to look like an idiot.

"Is that all right with you, Teal?" Mama searched my eyes for where I'd gone, smiling like June Cleaver for the company.

"Oh...yeah. Yes, I mean. That's fine. Um, are you ready now, Mr. Cian—um, Will?" I stretched my hand out, moving it about like it would help me find the words somehow.

"His stuff is in the squad car," the officer answered for him. "I can give ya both a lift over there if ya want."

"Sounds good." I lied once again, cringing at the thought of being in the back of a police car with the father of a missing child.

"Terrific," Mr. Limeberry interjected with too much gusto for the moment. I think he forgot that a child was missing and only remembered that he'd saved the day, and gotten another jewel in his crown as King of the greater South Carolina coast. He probably wanted us all to clap for him or commence the singing of "For He's a Jolly Good Fellow." "You treat Mr. Cianciola just like family, now, Teal."

I nodded as Officer Smathers motioned for Mr. Cianciola to proceed out of the door. I started to follow him, but Mr. Limeberry motioned to me for a sidebar. He waved his hand wildly toward himself, that fat-faced grin. He looked like Santa Claus calling a child back over for an extra treat after he'd already hopped off of his lap.

"Psst." He looked around to be sure the other two men had gone out the door.

"I really appreciate this, Teal. Look, Will

Cianciola is my best contractor. I hope he can hold it together and come back to work for me in the end. This is just terrible, but I really don't want to lose a good man, ya know? You take extra good care of him and I'll see to it that you're compensated."

"I appreciate that, Mr. Limeberry," I forced.

"You're a smart girl, Teal. I know you'd like to make something out of those little beach treasures of yours. Maybe this will give ya a little seed money. I hate this investigation is disrupting your workshop down on the shoreline. I tell ya what else," he smiled and put his hand on my shoulder. "I've got some private property just off of Hilton Head Island. There's nothing really there, just a little storehouse I built myself. But shells, driftwood, and everything you can imagine washes up down there. I'm happy to let you go sift through that sand all you want once this is all said and done with. Then you'll be able to start your little side gig and get on out of here. I know you want to."

"No, Mr. Limeberry, I—"

"But keeping after Mr. Cianciola, first, okay? We got a deal?"

And even though I wasn't sure just how involved I wanted to get in nursing a missing person's sad family member back to health, I smiled at my boss and nodded "yes."

When we got to the cottage, the officer and I

walked the luggage to the door while Will hung back to smoke a cigarette by the squad car. My guess? He hadn't smoked in years, since he was a teenager maybe. The stress of the situation had done it to him. He was just slightly more disheveled than a clean cut man on vacation ought to be, hair neatly trimmed, but not fixed, a young beard peering up out of normally cleanly shaved skin.

"Teal," the officer paused and set down the suitcase. "Teal, I think you should know that this is a criminal investigation. We don't have reason to believe this little girl just wandered off. There's evidence that suggests otherwise. Foul play, I'm afraid. So, you should be cautious. I assured your mama that you'd be safe, and that I'd personally see to it. But be smart, okay?"

"What kind of evidence?" A gruesome scene of mussed up sand, tiny smeared footprints, lonely bits of clothing…and blood, flashed through my mind's eye.

"I'm sorry, but I can't disclose any of that to you." He paused, and tried to rearrange his stiff expression into something a bit less ominous. "We're hopin' for the best here, but we are investigatin' a kidnappin'. It's been several weeks already. We have guys draggin' the marshes and checkin' in dumpsters. Do you understand what I'm sayin' to ya?"

"I think so…" I nodded. "What about her mama? Does Will have a wife or anybody?"

"His ex-wife left him when Chloe was just a toddler. She lives somewhere abroad and hasn't been back to the U.S. in years as far as we know. We're tryin' to contact her now. We haven't had very much luck with that."

"But if she'd been here, you'd know because of her passport, right? It would show up in the system or somethin', wouldn't it?" I probed, almost *hoping* her mother had been here. Maybe that was better than some stranger having taken her, or better for me somehow.

"Right." Officer Smathers paused. "But no need to worry yourself too much. We've got lots of people on this. We haven't ruled *anyone* out yet, in her disappearance. You're doing a good thing here, but keep your eyes open. If you're helpin' out over here at the cottage, make sure someone knows where you're at. Be smart. Don't try to play detective. Don't get paranoid, neither. Just be aware."

"Is Will one of the people you haven't ruled out yet?" I asked directly.

"Of course, it's common sense. He's the father, but like I said, we haven't ruled *anyone* out yet. I mean he's a guy from a rough area, who grew up as a street fighter. He doesn't have a great family background, but not terrible either. It's the typical father-ran-out-on-the-mother scenario, periods of poverty, stepdads in and out of his life…you know, *that* situation. He never got into too much trouble, just a couple little things here and there… but he's not squeaky clean, either. So just, like I said, keep your eyes open when you're around here."

"Should I be worried about bein' alone with Mr. Cianciola?" The thought occurred to me for the first time.

"I'm not sayin' that."

"You're not *not* sayin' it either."

"I've said what I can say, and maybe too much all ready. I've known Tracy my whole life, and I love this town. I just want you to be safe. That's all I've got for you, Teal." He looked past my shoulder and shot me a look that told me not to answer back.

"Mr. Cianciola, I think you're all set." Officer Smathers said in a more upbeat tone, still communicating to me from inside his sun-sculpted crow's feet. "Can I help you with anything further today, sir?"

When Will shook his head, Smathers nodded with a small smile and made his way back to the car. The whole thing felt weird, like I ought to tip him or something. Everything was weird about this. But then, I thought, how do you act when there's a little girl missing? Was there a normal way? Was there some type of missing child decorum I needed to know about? It's probably not something Emily Post covered in the etiquette book. Not that I would have read it if there had been. I actually profoundly hated *any* girl who ever cited Emily Post, although I'd gone to school with plenty of the sort. Afterall, it was still Charleston County, the home of manners and side glances.

I fiddled with the key for too long while I was lost in thought about everything I'd just learned. The lock was full of sand and moisture, and I could feel the metal grinding in a way that made my teeth gnash together. Will didn't seem to notice the noise, let alone anything else moving around him. He just stood in the late-summer heat, letting the sweat fall like overweight tears down his chiseled face. He was a little too good-looking for an old sad guy. But maybe he wasn't all that old…less than 40, for sure. He was what I'd always thought was old, but maybe not so much anymore.

The door popped open, and the humid room greeted us both with a salty musk. I couldn't smell a trace of the other travellers who'd been there before. Only the ocean's scent invaded the place, and it drowned out everything else. The ocean had a way like that. It would spill into a place and cancel out anything else that had been there, and declare its dominance. "It'll feel—and smell—a little better in here once I get the air up and runnin' for ya," I assured him, though I rather liked the odor.

"It's fine. I don't care." He shuffled in, leaving his bags piled up on the porch, and plopped down on the sand-stained '90s floral print couch.

"I'll get your bags," I said hurriedly.

"Leave them," he almost hissed.

"Okay." I froze.

He ran his hands through his dark hair that only had a streak or two of gray, almost unnoticeable. "I'm sorry. I don't know why I said it like that. I—I know you're just doing your job."

"It's all right." I whispered as smally as I could, aware of all the exit points in the room. "Can I do anything else for you? Anything at all? Have you eaten anything today?" I prayed he'd say yes and that I could leave.

He nodded. "I had half a bagel this morning. The cop practically shoved it down my throat in between questions I'd already answered a hundred times. That's all I can stomach for now."

I nodded, knowing better than to offer him anything else.

He stretched out on the couch and turned his body toward the back support, burying his face in between the pillows and the cushion, obviously not bothered that I was still standing in the middle of the room like some kind of displaced furniture. So, I took my cue. I made my way to the porch and quietly shoved his bags just inside the threshold using my foot. Then I shut the door behind me, and for whatever reason, ran like hell across the street, got inside my house, and dead bolted a door that hadn't been locked in years.

CHAPTER 3

I had dinner on the table when Mama got home that evening; nothing too special, just smoked sausage chopped up in a mess of fried-up sauerkraut. But at least we would eat. Mama worked the standard 9 to 5 like all the other mothers, but never seemed to have enough energy to fire up the stove when she got home. I was plenty old enough to fend for myself, of course, but I hadn't always been. And if I'd left it up to her, Huck would have eaten peanut butter and crackers for every meal. I got sick of them, myself, growing up. So I learned to make a small handful of dishes that are pretty hard to screw up. There were the standard spaghetti, sloppy joes, hot dogs, and frozen pizzas at first. Then I eventually graduated to crock pot soups and the special occasion roasts on holidays. But that night, chopped up meat on a bed of soured cabbage it was, and the stink of it fit just perfectly.

My mind was reeling from the events of the day like film from a horror movie. The flyer, the warnings from Officer Smathers, the desperate look on Will Cianciola's face. Then I'd made the mistake of Googling the little girl when I got home. At first it was just news stories that all said the same things, basically the facts from the flyer, and that there were no leads. But then I kept clicking link after link, and I ended up in some rabbit hole that led to a sick Wonderland with no Alice to lead the way. It was peppered with the faces of all sorts of missing children like little black specks over the top of a lump of mashed potatoes. Then came the educational sites and the statistics. None of it made me feel any better. If anything, the facts all came together and made a big dark cloud over the top of my head that didn't plan on leaving anytime soon.

I learned that if Chloe actually had been abducted and hadn't been found in the first four hours that she was most likely not to be found alive, and that a family member was the most likely culprit. I learned that another kid is reported missing every 41 seconds, and 20 out of a hundred children reported to the National Center for Missing and Exploited Children in non-family kidnappings will not be found alive. The statistics, the little girl's face, and the smell of the eerie salt breeze played tag with one another inside my head, all the players bouncing off the corners of my skull as if to squawk, "You're it! You're it! You're it!" from every corner.

I wished I could just go back and unlearn it all. I also wished I'd never been on the beach that night. Even if it turned out that I hadn't seen anything, I still felt connected, like maybe the moon and the tide had worked together to cast some sort of cosmic spell on me that attached me to Chloe Cianciola. I couldn't shake her. What was it? Paranoia? Concern? Reality, fantasy? I was *nobody*. I wasn't the kind of person who could have seen something worth seeing. They'd think I was an idiot kid playing detective if I started throwing out guesses based on nothing. Why was I stressing about this like it was my problem?

"Teal, I'm home." For once I was relieved to hear my mother's voice pipe up and warp me back to the smell of the sizzling polish sausage. I was about to burn it.

"Hey, Mom."

"I'm beat," she said with half a smoker's cough. She sat a clingy Huck down into the kitchen chair. "You're gettin' too damn big to be carried, son."

"How was your playdate today, buddy?" I asked him, spooning some of the crispy concoction onto a plate.

"Fine." He shrugged and threw down a crab

made out of a paper plate and orange pipe cleaners. "For you. Gage's mom had us make 'em."

"Aww, I love it, Huck! Thank you so much." I set down the spoon and looked it over like I'd just been handed an original Picasso. The oddly placed mouth and eyes matched the style.

"Huck," Mama sliced in, "why don't you find a good place for the crab to live in Teal's bedroom?"

"All right. Maybe on the mirror? I bet he'll sit tucked into the corner!" He beamed.

"Sounds good." I winked before his mosquito-bitten legs trotted out of the kitchen.

"Listen, Teal," Mama began, leaned up over the table, the second Huck was out of earshot. "I couldn't really say everythin' I wanted to say today with Officer Smathers, Mr. Limeberry, and not to mention, Will Cianciola, all, standin' there with us. But I need you to be *very* careful while this stuff is goin' on. Smathers promised me he'd keep an eye on you; it's the only reason I agreed to it. Not to mention that Limeberry owns us. But, just do your job and try to keep Mr. Cianciola comfortable. That way Limeberry gets his pat on the back from the boys in blue for helpin' out, and we keep our jobs. God forbid he do any *real* work himself. But, don't get too close to this case. Don't try to make friends with him or involve yourself in any way. Things like this can be real dangerous, you know what I mean?"

"I know, Mama. I won't involve myself. Don't worry about it." I set a plate down in front of her.

"I don't think ya get it, Teal. This was a kidnappin'. This was a criminal, who is still out there, probably a damn child molester or killer, who came into *our* town and took a kid. Things like that don't happen around here."

"I know someone took her. And it's a terrible thing, but isn't it usually the other parent actin' out in a custody battle or somethin'? That's what the internet says. The cops say that Will's ex lives in another country and hasn't been here in a long time. But I'm not so sure." I paused and pushed out a flash of the face from the beach trying to squeeze in on me. "I mean…this is *Folly Beach*. It's safe around here. Don't you think maybe her mama snuck back to get her or somethin'? I mean, she could have used a fake name or anything. And we don't know why she and Cianciola split up. Maybe the girl should be with her mother. Do you really think something *that* sinister really happened?" I tried to convince myself harder than anyone that everything was fine.

"I do. I—I think it could be linked to human traffickin' maybe. You hear about these sex rings all the time, you know. They're everywhere."

"Okay, Officer Benson. I think you've been watchin' too many Law & Order: Special Victims Unit reruns on your day off." I rolled my eyes.

"Should I set an extra spot at the table? Is Ice-T about to join us for dinner and questioning?"

"I didn't just come up with that, Teal." She raised her voice slightly. "I overheard Officer Smathers talkin' to Limeberry about it. You know they're thick as thieves. I couldn't make out exactly what they were sayin', but I heard enough of it. The police haven't gone public because they didn't want to cause panic in the coastal communities, but this isn't the first time a kid's gotten snatched. There've been two other kidnappin's, one a boy, and one a girl, in the past six months. Same m.o., kid grabbed on the beach durin' peak tourist weeks. Gone without a trace…just evidence of a struggle. One was in Myrtle Beach, and the other was somewhere around Hilton Head Island. They were mumblin' somethin' about these kids gettin' sold to bidders. After I heard that, they walked too far away, and I couldn't make anything else out. But I know what I heard, and it sounded real bad, Teal. I mean, there could be some kind of operation here. Don't you remember…there was a couple that tried to snatch a teenager from the Mount Pleasant Walmart about six months back? I'm tellin' you now, they're everywhere. A new kid is missin' every time I go open the Facebook." She popped a piece of the sausage into her mouth and watched me for my reaction.

"Oh my God." I put my hands to my head. "That makes me sick to my stomach. Who could possibly want to *purchase* a six-year-old child? It's bad enough with teenagers and grown women, but we're talkin' about a kid who probably still wets the bed."

"Apparently, kids that young and younger are in high demand. I heard them sayin' somethin' about Chloe bein' prime age for it. I don't even want to think about what on Earth for. It makes me want to throw up." She shook her head, her large gold hoop earrings bouncing off her jaws.

I tried to rub the goosebumps off my arms but just made them worse.

"But, Teal, these rings can run deep. It could be anybody you see on the street. Sometimes even parents sell their own children and stage the kidnappins. I've seen it on the news. It happens in normal places with normal people. It isn't always going on in some back room in another country."

"Do they suspect Mr. Cianciola?" I asked her flat out, my arms crossing over my body, both emphatic and protective.

"I don't know, but I think they always take a look at the father. Men are such scum, ya know." She sucked the grease off her skinny fingers. "But to tell ya the truth, Teal, I don't think they have the foggiest idea who all is behind it. So just be careful. If it is sex traffickin', or any kind of traffickin', then you don't want to get caught up in the cross hairs of it. Its roots are probably long and organized. Just keep away from it, whatever you do. All right?"

"I understand." I nodded as "Uncle" Hank stumbled through the back door.

"Wha—what d-do you understand, youngin'?" He slurred through his ratty salt and pepper goatee. "I betcha, no-not much a nothin'."

"Good god. Are you already wasted?" She glanced at me. "See, scumbags. I swear to god, Hank Feller. It ain't even 5:30." Mama shook her head and gritted her smoke-stained teeth.

"You swear to god, what, woman?" He got right up in her face.

"Go wash yourself up. You stink. And Teal has dinner ready," she said, dodging his breath.

"I don't give a goddamn what Teal has ready. Do-don't t-tell me what to do. I ain't your bitch." He growled like a foaming bulldog.

"Mama," I said, my heart pounding all the way into my ears. "Mama, he looks worse than usual. Look how dirty his overalls are. He's clearly been stumblin' and fallin' all over the place. Just leave him alone. He'll waddle off to the bedroom to sleep it off in a minute. Just stay out of his way, okay?" I spoke carefully, watching him amble around, pulling and fidgeting with his abnormally dirty work clothes.

"Yeah, bitch. Stay outta my way. Kid ain't half as dumb as she looks." Hank mumbled directly into the side of Mama's face, pulling her head hard against his reeking mouth.

She jerked away hard, shoving him in the chest with all her might.

"You done fucked up, now." He sneered and grabbed her by the elbow as she tried to dart away from his calloused grasp.

"Let her go. Right now. Let her go!" I screamed, eyeing the pot on the stove, and the heavy stirring spoon still in my hand.

"Mama!" Huck screamed out as he came running in frantically from the other room.

It seemed to all happen at once—my scream, Mama's, Huck's. It was the kind of clamor one would expect at a rock concert where no one knew how to play any of the instruments. I guessed that's how the song would go, though, if written about a family like ours...loud, disorganized, chaotic.

"I'll teach you to mouth off at me." Hank reared back and spit at her, still twisting her arm violently behind her back.

"What, Hank? You gonna hit me now? You gonna hem me up like this and pop me one? Do it, you coward!" Mama dared him.

Hank swung at her and missed her face, hurling his body toward the hot stove eye where his fist ultimately landed. When it did, his other arm released her, and he let out a guttural yell. "Son of a bitch! That's hot as hell! What idiot left the damn stove goin'?"

"Hank, Hank are you all right?" Mama tried to look at his already-blistering knuckles as he jerked them away.

"Just leave me the hell alone," he hissed, but more quietly, before he shot off toward the bedroom.

"I better get him some ointment or that's gonna be nasty once he sobers up." Mama said like she was just commenting on the weather or something. "I think I've got some aloe vera in the medicine cabinet."

"Are you kiddin' me?" I asked, tears streaming down my face. "He just tried to beat the shit out of you but was just too drunk to see it through. Now you're gonna run in there and help him lick his wounds?"

"Teal…" She lowered her eyes.

"Well, no thanks. I'm not interested in stayin' here to watch it. Come on Huck, we're goin' out for ice cream." I grabbed my little brother's sticky hand.

"Teal…Teal…he can't help it. He isn't like that when he's sober, and you know it. He's good to me when he's right in the head. He's just got this damn drinkin' disease. We need to help him get back on the wagon. Then we can be a real family. That's what families do, they…they help each other through messes like this. He didn't even hit me…he's just ornery. He tells me how much he loves me, and you kids, all the time, really."

"Haven't you heard, Mama? Sometimes love ain't enough. They even wrote a song about it once." I paused in the doorway and shook my head in some mix of disappointment and disbelief. "Come on, Huckie. We're gettin' out of here."

"But, Teal!" he cried. "I'm scared! I don't want to leave her!"

"I never do either, Huckie, but sometimes you've gotta." I smoothed his messy hair. "Come on. I'll get you some ice cream. We all need a minute to breathe, and there's no air left in here."

CHAPTER 4

The last few fishermen were packing up and leaving by the time we made it down to the pier.

The *thud, thud, thud* of a Yeti cooler leaving with its belly full of ice and choking fish matched the beat of Huck's little feet marching over the wooden slats. He was trotting along so innocently beside me, so unknowing of the danger that caused my insides to churn like the water that was just as unsettled only a few feet underneath us.

Maybe I'd made the wrong choice, running out of the house alone with everything that had been going on in town—an open child abduction case, for crying out loud—then the worse choice of turning onto the pier when I noticed that we were being trailed. There was no way off of it now, but if push came to shove, we could always jump off the side. We'd survive it; it wasn't all that high. I could grab

Huck and leap, then swim us in if it came right down to it. I'd do what I had to do. The commotion would scare off our tail, and we'd be all right.

I looked back.

"Don't you dare turn up onto this pier," I said to the figure behind me. "Just keep on walkin'."

I'd first noticed something was wrong at the cafe on Center Street. A shadow was lurking around outside, while Huck took a hundred years to pick out his ice cream toppings, all of which ended up being different versions of sprinkles. After I paid with the wadded up ten from my back pocket and ran out without my change, I thought I'd seen the figure turn the other way, inland, back toward the houses. That's why I went toward the water...where I had no outlet.

The pier was always full of tourists and fisherman until late evening in the summertime. But the clouds had started looking a little bit ominous, and the wind was already turning the palm leaves inside out. Nature had stood up flexing its big scary muscles and had just about run everybody clear off. It gave its fair warning, and let us everyone know what it had planned. And the crowd had listened. Huck and I were alone. Almost.

A stranger turned onto the old boardwalk, not half a football field behind me, and I froze up like a threatened rabbit on the side of the highway. I had a decision to make: pick up Huck and try to walk back, right past him, going back to the place I last felt safe, and hope for the best...or leap right off the edge of the pier. Flee the threat.

While I considered my options, the stalker inched closer. It was decision time. I scrambled for a moment. Left, then right.

"Let's go, Huck."

"I don't wanna go home yet," he whined. "I still have most of my ice cream left. And what if Uncle Hank is still there? You said we needed a break, anyhow."

The figure drew closer, quickening its pace to a jog.

"Right now, Huck." I reached out for his arm but wasn't quick enough.

"I said no, Teal!" He took off in a dead sprint toward the wrong end of the pier.

"Huck! Get back here!" I ran behind him. "Right now!"

"Teal!" A man called from behind me. "Teal, wait!" He caught up to me and then passed me all together. The fog was thickening and the lights on the pier were burnt out. I tried hard to keep my eyes on Huck.

"Stay away from him!" I shouted.

"Hey!" He yelled, this time directly at Huck, just before grasping his arm. "Stop!"

"Let him go!" I screamed. "Now!" I demanded frantically.

"Okay, okay," Mr. Cianciola responded, his hands outstretched like a police negotiator. "I was just trying to help you catch him...I...it's not...after what I'm going through, it freaked me out, a kid running off like that. Calm down. I was just trying to help you out."

"He was running towards an empty pier. You expect me to buy that?" I folded my arms against my shaken body.

"I wasn't thinking. I just saw him take off and I acted." He panted.

"Yeah, right. You've been following us since we were at Dolce Banana, haven't you? You were the creep trailin' behind us. Huck wasn't even runnin' from me then. I'm gonna call Officer Smathers." I patted at my pockets for my phone that I knew I'd left at the house.

"I—I was following you, but not since the ice cream store. It was actually since you left your house." He sighed, moving his hands back by his side.

"What!?" I hissed and pulled Huck closer to my leg where he was now clinging.

"I heard, uh, everything that was going on over there." He glanced at Huck, then back at me. "All the...the, uh, commotion, I suppose. I was asleep on the couch and woke up to it. I was worried, well, considering everything. Then I went out on the porch to listen, and I noticed it was coming from your house. That's when I saw you run out with him, looking all upset. I didn't know where you were going off to by yourself, with it getting dark so soon. I didn't know what had happened, or if you were hurt or something. I saw you had the kid with you. I was just trying to look out for you. Scout's honor. I—"

"Well, we're fine. You can see that. But I'm still gonna let Officer Smathers know you were followin' us around town. I don't care what you say." I clutched Huck's hand so tightly that he winced a little bit.

"Oh…I get it." He narrowed his eyes a touch. "Well, you take care, then. Sorry for the inconvenience."

"You get what?" I demanded as he tried to walk away from me.

"It's always the dad, right?" He shook his head and leaned onto the pier railing, just staring at me, waiting for some kind of reaction. It was almost as if he wanted me to say something to make him feel more awful, to help him twist the knife so that he wouldn't have to do it himself. He wanted to be tortured.

"I don't know what it always is," I said. "I don't know anything about any of this. I just wish I was far away from it."

"Of course you don't. Nobody does. And what are you? Nineteen? Twenty? It's normal to be scared. You were just thrown into being my little concierge because you're the low man on the totem pole. It's worse than shoveling elephant shit at the circus, being close to something like this. There's serious shit going on around you, and I get that. But it still sucks to have everybody looking at me like that. So just throw me a bone, all right?" Now he was torn between begging for both torture and grace.

"Why don't you watch your mouth around my brother? He hears it enough at home." I still gave him nothing.

"Sorry," he answered like it exhausted him.

I folded my arms, still guarding myself. Then I heard the slightest gasp come from his prominent throat, and saw the smallest sparkle on his cheek that the last bits of setting sun wouldn't let him hide. And I almost uncrossed my arms. I almost said something different than what I said, but I couldn't.

"I'm really sorry about everything, but I'm just interested in doing my job. Please don't *look out* for us anymore."

His answer was a nod, but a unique one. It spoke, and whatever it said was sad to hear. He paired it up with a scoff, like rich people pair red wine with filet mignon. They fit together perfectly.

"Let's go, Huck." I pulled at his little arm.

"But we just got here, Teal! I want to look for dolphins before we go. We always look for dolphins!" He pled.

"Not tonight."

"But, why not!?" He launched an innocent protest, oblivious to everything that had just happened. He was more innocent than I'd ever been. I'd always sensed whatever was going on around me, and it had been a curse.

"You should listen to your sister, little man." Will spoke to him, then looked at me. "You never know who might be hanging around here at night."

I held his gaze for just a second longer, then grasped Huck's arm even tighter, and dragged him off the pier.

CHAPTER 5

Huck had given up his outcry and was asleep in my arms by the time I got back to the house.

Hank was nowhere in sight, nor was his 20-year-old half red Ford pickup truck. Still, I felt the need to put Huck in my room instead of in his own for the night. I liked to have him close by so I could look after him on the nights when Mama and Hank had been into it; at least I thought it was to look out for him. But maybe not. Maybe there wasn't any truly good deed that wasn't just a little selfish somewhere deep down. Maybe I didn't want to be alone because I was scared too. I didn't really know, and in that moment, didn't have the strength to mull it over. I was spent.

I carried his wormy sprawled out body into my bedroom and flopped him down into my unmade bed. Then I tucked him in nice and tight and whispered, "Snug as a bug in a rug," before I kissed his clammy forehead. After that, I made my way across the house to Mama's room for the check-in I had dreaded the whole way home. This was the time of night I'd go make sure she was okay, and then she'd passionately defend the scumbag while I bit my tongue. I was surprised I had a single taste bud left by the time I got through school.

When I came around the corner I expected to find the lights cut out and then to see her still-clothed body passed out on top of that old ratty quilt some great aunt had made. Next, I'd go through my little routine—make sure she was breathing, put a glass of water in her reach, and turn her on her side in case she puked. But this time it was different. I found the lights on, a couple gnats clinging to the yellow bulb in the middle of the old ceiling fan. Her suitcase was thrown out on the bed, and she was jamming unfolded clothes into it while tears streamed down her mascara-run face that looked like some worn out version of my own.

"What are you doin'?" I asked, my eyebrows moving up to high alert.

"I'm leavin' for a day or two. I need a break from the madhouse. I'll take Huck with me so you can hold down the fort at the office without him in tow. Hank Feller is on the warpath again. I just need to get out of here till it all settles down. Put my ass in the sand and problems in the wind." She spoke about a hundred miles an hour.

"You're just gonna get Huck up outta the bed, take off, and leave me here by myself?" My voice went up a good octave.

"Hank has never given you a second thought. If I'm not here, he ain't comin' within a thousand miles of this place. You'll be fine. Plus, we can't both leave Limeberry high and dry. He'll cut us loose. Then what will we do? Limeberry Properties is our home, our food, our everythin'." She flitted around like a maniac, all out of breath and twitchy.

"I'm not worried about that dumbass Hank Feller, Mama. I'm worried that there's a major child-nappin' case bein' investigated right underneath our noses. Right across this narrow-ass single-lane street we *live* on, to be exact. I don't exactly want to be alone here right now. You even told me to watch my back earlier tonight. I get that you're hurt, and I'm glad you're comin' to your senses on that one. But, do somethin' else! Call the cops on him. Get a restrainin' order. Hell, let's all pack up and go. We could work at another Limeberry Property."

"You know he won't let us transfer. And I don't want to get the police involved, have all of 'em knowin' my business. Plus, they've got enough on their plate right now. I doubt they'd spend too much time worryin' about Hank Feller."

"It feels like you're just gonna up and leave me here while you go take some sort of mini-vacation!"

"It's hardly a Sandals Resort, Teal. I just need a mental break."

"But—"

"I'll let Smathers know you're here in the mornin'. Keep the doors locked. Have a friend or somethin' stay over if you don't wanna be alone. You're a tough girl, practically grown now. I just meant for you not to go nosin' around that case. It ain't gonna come lookin' for ya. Don't be so paranoid. You ain't nobody special, darlin'." She started crying harder, and looked at me head on, revealing the other side of her face. "We can't lose our jobs and our home. But if I stay, I'm afraid he'll come after me." She paused and pursed her fat lips. "It was real bad this time. Different. I'm glad you and your brother weren't here to see it."

"Dear God," I gasped, and took a step closer. "You need to see a doctor."

"It's fine," she pulled her hair over the side of her face.

"It isn't fine, Mama. Your cheek ain't even settin' right. And your eye is swollen plumb shut. You won't even be able to see to drive like that! You can't go anywhere tonight!"

"I can see fine through my other eye. I'll manage. I always manage." She stormed past me, toward Huck's room, with her suitcase in hand.

"You're actin' crazy!" I said. "You don't even sound like yourself right now. Just calm down and think logically for a minute, won't ya? Why not call the cops and have them pick his sorry ass up? I know they have a big case, but they still have to do their jobs. Isn't that more practical than skippin' town torn all to hell in the middle of the night with your seven-year-old son?"

"What? File a report, tell people that we personally know all of our business, and have a bunch of embarassin' pictures taken? Then what, Teal? They throw Hank Feller in the can for two nights, and then it's even worse because we've pissed him off? No thanks. I prefer it my way, thank ya. I've always been able to take care of myself."

I said nothing.

"I'm tellin' ya, Teal, it'll blow over. I just gotta get out. Get some sun and a good margarita. That's what I need."

"Then leave Huck here, and go do you for a few days."

"You can't work extra shifts and look after Huck. Limeberry won't even let me bring him to the office if he's sick. And we sure as hell can't afford to pay a sitter more than we already have to. He's gotta come with me. He'll build sandcastles and mind his business. It'll be fine."

"Well, where are you plannin' on goin'?" I demanded.

"Up to a vacant property. Surfside Beach, just below Myrtle. It's less than two hours. It won't be a bad drive, but Hank won't bother to make it." She lowered her voice to a whisper, but a rushed one when we made it to my room.

"I just wish you wouldn't do this." I felt helpless as I watched her scoop up Huck's sleeping limp body.

"How many wishes you ever had come true?" She stopped and eyed me with the one that was still open. "I've gotta jet, girl."

"So what about when you come back? Are you just gonna take Hank back and act like none of it ever happened? Give him time to cool down, and then start the routine all over again? He could have killed you, Mama! Next time he might finish the job!"

"God, Teal…I don't know." She squeezed the air like it was my neck. "You think you could get off my back for once and just let me process it? I don't have all the answers right now."

"Whatever." I rolled my eyes.

"Keep the doors locked. We'll be back in no time," she said in a tone that told me she wasn't going to discuss it another second.

I just shook my head and shrugged my shoulders.

I leaned in and kissed Huck on his sweaty temple that hung over her equally sweaty tank top. And though every part of my body was screaming at me to stop her, I let them go. At seventeen, her word tied my hands. But to this day, I wish I'd fought her. I wish I'd wrestled her to the ground and stolen Huckie back from her. Because that night, by standing there, decorating the scene like a second-hand throw pillow, not really doing much of anything at all, I made the biggest mistake of my life. I let them go to Surfside Beach that night.

CHAPTER 6

I barely slept at all the night Mama and Huck left for the stretch of beach that was two hours north of ours. I think I finally just gave in sometime around 4:30 a.m. My mind was strong, but my body eventually reserved its right to override the system and shut it all down. I only wished it would have done it sooner. When my alarm rang at 7:00 it felt like it'd been about fifteen minutes of that kind of half sleep you get on a school field trip. You drift, but never quite leave shore for fear one of the other kids is going to draw on you with permanent marker or stick your hand in a cup of warm water. It barely qualified as sleep at all.

I hit snooze once, coveting that extra eight minutes, but knowing it wouldn't really help anything. I had to be at work by 8:00…I was known to get by with 8:15, but that was it. Sometimes that's the hardest part of the whole damn day was getting out of bed, accepting that first cold chill and acknowledging the warmth of my bed was gone.

I didn't mind waking up at all hours of the night if I had to go fossil hunting. Low tide happened when low tide happened. And it was nothing to me, because I wanted to do it. If I could have been on some faraway beach I'd only known about thanks to Google like Borre, Denmark, or Western Cape, South Africa, I'd always be searching for the amazing things the Earth had left behind—my truest passion—I don't think I'd ever have needed to sleep at all. But, getting up at the crack of dawn to go sit in an office that reeked of old ink toner didn't get me too fired up. I longed to wake up for something I *wanted* to do. Surely someone somewhere did. Couldn't I?

"Some way to spend that *magical* summer after senior year." I groaned out loud, turning the alarm off. "And of course, no call. No courtesy to tell me you got there safely. Thanks a lot, Tracy."

I scrolled down through the recent calls to Mama's number and dialed. About four seconds later I heard her obnoxious ringtone, some old hair band song, bouncing and vibrating from the kitchen table. *Great.* I tossed my phone down onto the comforter, cutting Bret Michaels off before he could ask me to talk dirty to him again.

"Glad you're concerned about me, Mama. Parent of the year, Tracy McHone." I spoke into the air, and then stumbled to the shower.

When I finally got out the door too close to 8:00, I was in a mad rush. I was trying to balance my lunch box (one of Huck's Ninja Turtle ones), purse, and three short-term rental agreements in my mouth while I locked the rusty deadbolt.

"Don't give me problems today, pleeeeease." I mumbled to the sticky lock with the papers tacked to my lips like a wet cigarette. After I finally sweet-talked the key back out, I turned around to dash to the golf cart when I saw it…the front door to Will Cianciola's place hanging as open as an all-night mini mart.

"Son of a bitch." I grumbled out loud, slamming down my armful of summertime blues, and spitting out the mouthful of paperwork. "I guess I get to be the one to check on it. Fan-freakin-tastic."

I quickly made my way across the puddled road, mad as all hell that his stupid door flapping in the morning breeze was about to make me *very* late for work when it occurred to me. Maybe this wasn't just some rush hour inconvenience. This was a man neck deep in a kidnapping scandal. He'd seemed innocent enough the night before, but maybe I didn't need to just go over there and shut the door for him like a good neighbor and go on my merry way. What if it wasn't just the wind that had blown it open? Maybe I needed to call Officer Smathers. It seemed that Will had been in a bad way the night before, a bad state of mind. Maybe he had found trouble. Maybe he *was* the trouble. My constant confusion over him made arguments both ways in my head, and the jury was at a stalemate.

I thought about it until I found my flip-flopped feet standing on his front porch, hesitating to go inside. I suppose some part of me had decided against erring on the side of caution. Was it my gut? I didn't know. But my head told me he did seem like a good guy, talking to him on the pier—he was in shambles for sure—but good. I'd seen bad. Hank Feller was bad. Will didn't seem like that to me, even though I'd been so cold to him. He was pissed, offended, probably half drunk…but not *bad*.

I eyed the windows looking for any sign of movement, a shadow behind the off-white sheer, the glow of a television…anything at all. I didn't step through the threshold, but called out "um—Hello? Will? Uh, your door is open. Are you in there?"

Nothing. I pulled out my cell phone, dialed 911, just in case, but didn't push send.

"Will, are you in there somewhere? Will!?" I shouted louder, rising up onto my blue-polished tiptoes.

Silence.

I peeked, once again, into the window to my right, and saw nothing really, just a disheveled but eerily still living room. A few lonely cigarette butts in an ashtray, some clothes on the floor, and a stack or two of newspapers strewn out across the floor was about all there was to look at. I relaxed for a brief moment until a huge gust of ocean wind slammed the screen door shut and back open again in an instant, triggering my finger to push send. I'd always heard that if you held an egg in one hand and a gun in the other, that it's impossible to smash the egg without pulling the trigger. Same concept. Apparently a frighteningly loud noise has a similar effect, because my thumb had never moved that fast before.

"9-1-1, what is your emergency?" Pause. "9-1-1, are you there? What is your emergency, please?"

"Teal?" Will stumbled out of the front door just then, shirtless, a ratty fleece blanket wrapped around his shoulders, with unruly hair and a five o'clock shadow. "What are you doing out here? What time is it?"

"9-1-1. Can you tell me your name and location?"

"Um, no emergency. I dialed by accident. Thank you." I hung up.

Will lifted his eyebrows as if to ask me, once again, what I was doing standing on his porch with such a frantic look on my face.

"Your door was opened. I—I was worried. After the state you were in last night, I was…concerned, I guess. I mean, I know how upset you've been. And that…the way I reacted to you made it worse." I stumbled but finally got there.

Will looked at the door, then at me. "Oh—I, uh—I stopped off and grabbed a twelve pack on the way back from the pier last night. Killed a few in the alley before I made it back. I guess I didn't shut the door behind me all the way. " He shrugged.

"You were just drinkin' in the alley by yourself all night?" I looked him up and down.

He paused, maybe to rummage around for an excuse, but relented quickly if that was the case. "What's the right answer to that, Teal? If I say yes, you'll give me that pitiful worried look I keep getting every fuckin' where, and if I say no, you'll know that I'm lying to your face. So I have to decide between which one of those sad sacks of shit I want to be this time. Hmm." He put his hand to his chin.

"I was just worried." I whispered.

He continued on as if he hadn't heard me. "Yeah, my daughter's been missing…for too long. I was drinking in the alley by myself. I drank nine of the twelve faster than I thought humanly possible, then stumbled back here, puked, and finished 'em off sometime between then and now. Most of that is pretty much a blank space now, to be honest with you." He nodded in some kind of ironic way as he regurgitated the evening to me. "So, that's why my door was hanging open and why I look like hell. But, please, if you have fresh towels for me, just go ahead and leave them by the door there. Let me see if I can rustle up a tip. I think I had 38 cents in my jeans pocket."

I couldn't decide if he was being a complete asshole, or if he was just putting me in my well-deserved place. It was true that however he wanted to spend his time was none of my business, but it was also true that I was just trying to be a decent person after I'd treated him like a criminal. I had to remember he was the victim, at least one of them. Either way, you don't see someone's door hanging open and just walk off, but you don't judge either. I thought about just walking away then, chalking my whole effort up as a lost cause, but instead I blurted, "Hank Feller beat the shit out of my mother last night, and she took off to a Limeberry property near Surfside Beach, and left me in the middle of whatever in the hell is going on around here. By myself. I'm not some doe-eyed kid trying to save you from yourself, nor am I some self-righteous piece of shit like I might have come off last night. I got worried because I saw something weird, and it freaked me out. I thought you could be in trouble. I might join you in the alley tonight. I'm sure as all hell not judgin' anybody. I'm just being a human." Then I turned around and trotted toward the road as casually as I could.

"Teal, wait…wait. I shouldn't have snapped at you like that." He caught up and took me gently by the arm. "Of course, you would have thought the open door was suspicious, all things considered. I—I know we're all dealing with stuff all the time. I just…I don't know what to do. It was just me and Chl—*her* for a long time." He couldn't say her name, and his pain in trying to say it and failing, somehow broke inside of my body like a thief into an abandoned house. And it hurt me too. I could feel it, the sadness, a tingle in the air that had somehow seeped into my pores.

"I'm sorry. I know what it is to be alone," I said. "And I know what it is to want to stay out all night by the water where at least the sound of the waves will keep you company…but also never talk back. The water is as restless as you are, but doesn't try to help. It just grumbles right along next to you. Great company for the miserable. I get it. Don't worry. I'll just mind my business from now on. I won't ask you any more questions."

He looked past me for a minute toward my house then asked, "Did he hurt you too?"

"Now you're askin' question." I sighed.

"Did he?"

"No." I shook my head. "Nothin' physical, anyway. *He's* never laid a finger on me." Some of the ones before Hank flashed through my mind.

"That's good. I'm sorry he worked on your Mom, though. It's a tough thing to see. My old man had a drinking problem. He was rough on my mother a lot." His accent thickened when he said it.

"Where are you from, anyway?" I avoided talking about Hank Feller any longer. "Cianciola isn't a name we hear around here. I know you said up north somewhere, and I can hear that much."

"The name's Italian. I'm half Italian, half Irish, which in South Boston gets your ass kicked by everybody. I grew up there, then moved over to Watertown after I got married. It was a little bit better than where I grew up, but not a whole lot."

"You look it." I nodded while I perused his dark hair and eyes, and just lighter-than-olive skin. "Italian, I mean. I always wanted tan skin like that. My tan is always gone by late September."

"Nah…you've got good skin. People pay for skin like yours." His face let me know how awkward he felt after saying that.

"Thanks…I—I gotta get to work now. Double duty with Mama gone. God, I'm so late." I looked down at my phone.

"Yeah, you better get going." He turned back

toward his house as I trudged off.

I had more words in my throat, but I wasn't sure what they might be. More mumbling about skin, perhaps? I didn't know why I felt this urge to turn around and holler something back to him, but I fought it, mainly because I couldn't come up with anything else to say. It was a strange feeling, and I didn't have the slightest idea what it was, but it felt like a magnet or a strong undercurrent…a big one pulling me in hard, too strong to fight.

CHAPTER 7

The next morning went better than the first after Mama took off with Huck. Sunrise was at 6:29 a.m., and it came almost perfectly with low tide. I knew I'd get some good beach finds if I was able to beat out the early morning storm that the weatherman had said would roll in by about 7:00. If I used my thirty minutes of prime hunting time wisely, I'd be done, have beaten Mother Nature, and arrive at work right on time. I knew I could scrape up a few treasures.

I made my way down the beach walk with my used tools stuffed into random pockets of my equally beat up overalls that I think had once belonged to one of the "uncles." The beach was foggy and humid, the breeze trying hard to ward off the heat that the Lowcountry trapped in its clutches at all hours that time of year. There was never a breeze quite strong enough, though. Not even hurricane force winds could cool off the dog days in late summer. I'd learned to live with it. It never stopped me from doing what I needed to, and that morning would be no different. As the first bead of sweat let go of the ledge of my eyebrow, I started to dig into the earth.

"Now I'm starting to think it's you following me," Will teased, his face shining tan through the ghostly fog. He seemed to be the one thing that could always manage to interrupt my life, harder to ward off than the heat.

"What are you doing out here, Cianciola? I hope to heaven above you didn't sleep out here. That shit is dangerous. About a drunk a year drowns from passing out on the beach at night and getting washed out at high tide."

"I thought you were through asking me questions," he replied.

I eyed him, my hands on my hips, my sanctimonious ways creeping back not so stealth-like.

"I didn't sleep out here." He relented, then took his voice up an octave. "I came to watch the storm roll in. I like beach storms, you know, finding moments of happiness where I can."

I let my hands fall back by my side. "You're out here looking for her." I regretted saying it the second it came out of my mouth.

Will smiled softly and made some noise that resembled a laugh, but wasn't one. It was the noise a person would make instead of holding up their hands and admitting guilt.

"God, I'm sorry. I blurt sometimes, I—"

"Don't be." Will gritted his teeth revealing deep dimples. "I look all the time. I just try not to bum everyone out by constantly talking about it you know? Not that many people want to talk to me, anyway."

"It doesn't bum me out." I shrugged, then felt my eyes get huge. "I mean, it does. I'm very bummed out…I'm just saying, it doesn't bother me to hear about it. So…talk."

He went on, to my surprise, after I sounded so awkward. "Okay…I wonder about every person I see around here. I stare at every man on the street dead in the eyes just to see if he gives anything away. Someone's got my daughter somewhere. And the first hours she was gone…" Will paused, and the fog was helping me to read his face. "Those first crucial hours, they weren't out looking for her. They had me in a box, shooting questions at me like a firing squad while I crumbled in the corner like a fucking scared dog. They asked me anything and everything, from if I "accidentally" spanked her too hard, or tried to stop her crying by holding something over her mouth, to if I *sold* her to someone. All the while, I felt like my chest was being clawed apart by bloodthirsty animals. I just wanted them to find her."

"I can't imagine what that would feel like. I'm so sorry." I stood up to see him better, my little gardening shovel still in my hand.

"They don't like where I come from or how I grew up. They're picking my life apart, trying to make their ideas about me work. Everybody I see looks at me like this Yankee out-of-towner with three heads, and they want to ask me the same damn things the cops did. They don't like my accent or my name. They get their little theories churning. You know. It's what you thought at first too."

I tried to shake my head but didn't all the way.

"So I look," he continued. "I do what I can, but now it's been almost a month. A *month*. And all I ever find are broken-ass bits of seashells."

"I—I don't know wh—"

"Honestly, I think it's why I followed you in the first place the other night. I wanted to play the hero, succeed at something by helping you out. It can be a distraction from what's going on in your own life, involving yourself in something that's none of your damned business. That's why I did it. The chaos I heard coming out of your house, for just a second, was louder than the chaos in my own head. I'm sorry. I owe you an apology too. Maybe I overstepped, just trying to find some other reason to keep breathing through all this. I was following you to see if you were okay, but hell, maybe to see if I was okay too. I don't know the whole reason. I don't know what I'm ever looking for anymore. I don't know if it's Chloe, or if it really was you that time. Maybe I'm looking for some part of me that's still alive. I don't know *what* I am possibly searching for every second of the day now."

I thought of myself when he said this, how I'd break my own bones keeping Huck safe, but wondering if it was really all for me. Maybe in keeping Huck close, I was comforting myself...or trying to fill up some void.

"It's been a hundred years, not just weeks." He was still pouring out. "Every day the same. Questions. No new developments. And I know the stats. I just don't know what to do. I feel helpless, and I'm her father. I should be able to do something. But I can't. So I walk around out here, just looking for....anything." His face was still calm, but his clenched knuckles had turned white.

I honestly couldn't tell if he was talking to me anymore or just talking, but I decided to respond anyway. I took a few steps toward him, over top of the tools strewn out on the packed sand. "I wish I knew what to say to you, but I don't. I do know how you feel though. I mean, not about your daughter—

no one could understand that unless they'd been there—but about not knowin' what to do, and just lookin' for everything and nothin' all at the same time. That part, I get. I always end up down here when everything is all screwed up. I'm looking for the same thing you are. *Anything.* You see, I'm from here. I see people venture out here to the beach or to the pier for every reason in the world. But you can bet that if it's after the sun has gone down, or before it's come up all the way, it's because they're searchin' for somethin' or another. It could be a lost weddin' ring, or hell, even treasure they've just heard legends about. But every time, every single time, it's for somethin' more than they can even put their own finger on. An answer that doesn't exist. Somethin' only God, himself, knows that they need. And it can't be done in the daylight. It's gotta be done when it's scary, and risky, and lonely—the hour when your soul comes out from hidin' from the light of day…when it has the balls to show up and bear it all. That's what you're out here lookin' for….your daughter, and everything else too."

He looked into my eyes, his like sea glass, dark and glistening, and he knew. He knew that I understood what it was to feel hopeless, to feel stuck, to feel shackled to this stretch of sand against my will. Even if my reasons weren't as big as his, I knew, and he could feel it this time; that thing in the air that crawls inside. My being able to understand was the help I had to offer that morning. It was the one arrow in my near-empty quiver. So he took it, having already used all his arrows. And we sat there, just knowing it together until the silence got too heavy, and one of us had to crack under its weight.

I took the bait. "But at least we're here. We're alive. We're breathin'. That's what matters." I went back to fiddling with my tools.

"Is that always the goal?" he added. "Just to stay alive, even if it hurts like hell? Hope for silver linings someday?" He all but scoffed in my face.

"I think it's damn well gotta be. If not, then it's all for nothin', right?"

"Maybe some things are just for *nothin.'*." He parroted my accent.

"I don't think so." I cocked my head sideways, looking up at him from my squatted position, my humidity-tousled curls tickling my shoulders. "It's like how the sand dollars are so pretty and perfectly symmetrical." I picked one up from beside his bare feet. "We find 'em when they're already dead and washed up. Worthless to the earth accordin' to some. But I think God made them pretty so we're drawn to pick them up and use them for somethin' good again."

"Whatever you say." He shrugged, but I could tell what I'd said made sense to him.

"I think it's why I have this little hobby of mine that I hope to turn into a business someday. I make fine jewelry out of the stuff I find on the beach or in the river beds around here. There's a woman in town who has taken me on as an apprentice. God knows, I don't have the money to pay for the equipment we use to dig for the good stuff, or for the jewels and gold we add on to them to make it fancy instead of that junk you'd find in a boardwalk gift shop. But I'd like to eventually make it bigger, buy into it maybe, get the whole nation wearing pieces of Folly Beach on their bodies. There's been a lot of ugly shit go down on this sand, so why not try to make what's left of it mean somethin'? This place should be known as somethin' better than Coffin Island. Maybe you've heard the legends....else you probably think I'm nuts." I focused back on the hole I was now rooting around in.

"Yeah...people disappearing. I've heard them. Lived them." He let out a nervous laugh and looked at me like I was crazy, but like he was also kind of amused.

I realized then that I shouldn't have said anything about the disappearing legends, but I was already committed now, so I treated him like a normal person and continued on with it. "Well, like I said, I just want to make what little good out of the wreckage that I can. Give it some purpose, you know? Everything has a purpose somehow. I promise. Even the bones on Coffin Island. It all matters."

He held my gaze, trying to decide if I was wise beyond my years or just some stupid kid spouting off at the mouth when the first crack of thunder sounded from somewhere out over the water.

"You'd better get your tools together there and get inside. It's about to come one. You don't want to be out here holding metal in a lightning storm." He said it as if I'd never heard as such.

"And what about you?" I asked, gathering up my things.

"I think I will watch the storm roll in, after all." He looked out toward the horizon.

"You're insane if you do it out here," I said as the drops shot down at us like stray bullets. "You're about to get pounded any second. Go watch it from your porch. Do you realize how bad the summer storms get down here, Yankee?"

"Kind of like *Fight Club*, isn't it? Sometimes you need a good beating to feel better. You're probably too young to catch that reference though."

"I'm not too young for anything." I flashed a smile. "Enjoy the storm then. I hope it hails for you, Tyler Derden." I paused for him to say goodbye, or perhaps something smartass, but he said nothing. So I took off running toward the boardwalk.

I was about halfway there when he called out, "Teal," competing against a crack of thunder.

I turned around to face him, but said nothing, the rain now beating my curls into straight spaghetti noodles.

"You want to grab a bite or something tonight? That way you don't have to be by yourself this evening, and maybe it'll keep me out of the alley with a twelve pack for one night. That is, if you're not too busy digging up carcasses to make necklaces out of or something."

I thought for a second, a rush of fear and excitement, and something else brand new drowning out the alarms. Whatever it was cued up my vocal chords to work again. Then it came out, despite all the warnings from Mama and Smathers…and from myself to keep my distance, "Sure. The Crab Shack. 7:00."

"See you there," he said and smiled all the way for the first time since I met him.

CHAPTER 8

Did I just make a date with Will Cianciola? I asked myself that question on repeat for half of the morning while scrolling too fast down my Instagram feed to really see anything. I'd get a glimpse of a Kardashian here and there, or a girl taking a photo of her own ass in a public bathroom mirror, but that was about it. But what else was there to do? It was a slow morning at Limeberry Properties, with only a couple of phone calls, and no check-ins. It always got like this when school was about to start up again. The office would grow unnervingly quiet soon, with only the occasional renter stopping in. Soon it would become only the mysterious winter beach goers who never wanted to be bothered...it was only halfway like that now. There were still a few people without school-aged children milling around, enjoying the less-crowded late season, risking the possibility for hurricanes. It was also just empty enough to keep my mind open, so Will Cianciola could stomp back and forth through it as he pleased with that sad and thunderous rhythm that always gave him away.

This was *not* going to be a date. What grieving father would even make a date? And with me, of all people? I was the glorified towel girl with skinny legs and barely-healed acne scars. He was lonely; that was all. He could tell we both needed the company. He was being nice.

But, there was just something *different* about the way he asked. Like the words had something behind them that he didn't even know they did. I scrolled some more, trying not to think about it. It worked for about twelve seconds while I wondered why any of these girls thought I cared where they bought the dress that they were wearing in front of one of the Rainbow Row houses downtown. Then he was back, traipsing through my head in heavy-ass work boots.

I told myself that I was just going for some companionship. It wasn't like I'd developed some sad crush. It wasn't like I was *attracted* to him. Right? Not that I would have known how to recognize it even if I had been. What's more, I didn't know if I'd ever really been on a date…I mean, possibly? I watched a movie at Hannah Clark's house with her boyfriend and a guy named Jake

Something, who, I guess was my date. Hannah told me to sit by him, and when it got dark he tried to put his hand up my skirt. Then there was the boy from that church camp Mama sent me off to so she could have a couple weeks alone with Uncle Mike…or Uncle Mark….Uncle Mack? Anyway, there was a boy I'd meet after hours and awkwardly French kiss. I can remember our tongues moving around in circles while I wondered how I would ever make it stop. It wasn't that I didn't like it; I did, to some extent. It was exciting and weird, and would sometimes make me feel the oddest hot tingle in my frayed jean shorts, especially when he'd climb on top of me and grind his weight against me a little bit, or would run his hand up my shirt and under my bra—as far as I'd ever let it go. But I was always so preoccupied with how I would end it. How would I just abruptly stop kissing somebody? How would he know when to take his hand out from under my flimsy tank top? I'm still not sure how we stopped, but I guess we just did at some point. It's not like I was still back there kissing the dude. Maybe there'd been a rustle in the bushes or a set of headlights coming down the dirt road…a mystery to likely remain unsolved.

That was about it—the extent of my experience with guys. At seventeen, I was starting to think that I might have been the only virgin left on Earth. I knew I was behind. Waaay behind. Most of the girls at my school had taken care of that by sophomore year. Here I was, graduated, should have been college bound, at least Trident Tech bound, and nothing. Maybe being stuck in the Limeberry office, smelling window air conditioners instead of riding around in those open Jeeps, had kept me honest for longer. Or maybe it had been looking at my mother's life and knowing that I didn't want it to become mine. It was probably a little of both. It's not like I'd never thought about it, or wanted it, or searched myself for it late at night…something I'd never admitted to. I just hadn't found the right person. I wasn't gonna get hard up enough to just give it away at the one party a year I might have made it to. Like everything else…I wanted magic. Ocean force, full moon, high tide, record-breaking waves…magic.

Why are you thinkin' about this now, Teal? Stop it. I tried to convince myself it was for no reason, just pesky little thoughts, while encouraging Will's slightly lined face to get out of my head…along with that semi-familiar and uninvited twitch in my jeans. *God.* I banged my head against the desk. What was wrong with me? He was a grieving father at least twice my age in the worst place of his life. And he wasn't even nice. Not even a close. But I wasn't sure I liked nice, anyhow.

"Teal, you all right?" A voice trespassed into my

thoughts.

I jumped up, flushed, as if he could see my private thoughts playing out like a movie in front of us. "Officer Smathers. Um...what can I do for you?"

"Are you okay, there? You seem kind of out of sorts. Did somethin' happen?" He looked me over good.

"No. I'm fine. Fine, fine, fine." I paused while he eyed me even more. "Truth is, it's awful slow around here. I'd about dozed off when you walked in. The door dingin' made me jump, is all. I thought maybe you were Mr. Limeberry comin' through. I'd hate to get caught bein' lazy on the job, ya know..."

"All right, then." He took his dark aviator sunglasses off, still looking me over closely.

"What brings you in today?"

"I'm lookin' for Hank Feller. You seen him lately?" He leaned onto my desk to look me in the face.

"Not since last night." I shook my head, surprised that he'd come in asking about Hank instead of Will. "He and Mama got into it, and I left the house. He was gone when I got back."

"Sumabitch prolly skipped town," Smathers said more to himself than to me.

"What's he done?" I asked, thinking, *other than to my mother*.

"Nothin' more than what he's always doin'.

Kickin' up dust and gettin' out before it settles. We just had some questions for him."

"Is it about him roughin' Mama up a little bit? Did a neighbor call or somethin'?" I asked before he turned around.

"Did he do somethin' to Tracy last night? Is she around here anywhere?" he asked, obviously hearing about it for the first time.

"I—I mean he knocked her around some. I thought—"

"He ever touch you or Huck, Teal?" He furrowed his brow.

I shook my head, no.

"Where's your Mama at?"

"I don't know, exactly. She and Huck went to stay at one of the other properties to hide out for a few days. Surfside Beach somewhere."

"Another Limeberry property?" he asked.

"Yeah. I mean, she couldn't afford to stay anywhere different."

"Well, that's good. Limeberry runs a tight ship. I'm sure she'll be all right there."

"I'm sure. She just needed a little break, I guess," I replied, wondering what all was going through his head, and more, what exactly he wanted with Hank Feller.

"All right, well…you just keep your eyes peeled and doors locked. There's a lot of movin' parts around here right now. If you see Hank Feller, don't tell him I came around askin' about him. You just give me a ring, all right?" His tone was different; stranger than it had been during our first meeting.

"I'll do it." I nodded.

"Thanks, Teal. You take care of yourself, now." Smathers tipped his hat and turned around.

"Officer Smathers," I stopped him, jogging out from behind the desk. "I have a lot of questions, but I don't know what they are. If you know what they are, I'd appreciate it if you'd give me the answers I need. I feel like there's all this commotion everywhere, but I just can't see any of it. And I'm more afraid that maybe I'm too close to it."

He sighed and just looked at me for a moment. "I think you're all right, Teal. But…there are a lot of people under suspicion right now, and a thousand details I can't tell you about. All I can say is that there's a hurricane makin' landfall. And you're right about one thing…you're awful close to where the damage could hit. It might miss ya, but I'd still board up my windows. We've got a big storm in a small area. You got it?"

"I think so." I swallowed hard and felt my heart try to break out of my chest.

"I'll be here. Don't you be fallin' asleep on the job, now. And again, let me know if you see Hank out and about."

"Of course." I answered, my voice impersonating an obedient soldier. "I'll be on the lookout. Wide awake, sir."

CHAPTER 9

I dressed up way too much. I shouldn't have worn the thin yellow sundress and sandals. I shouldn't have bothered to put the makeup on or the perfume, either. I never wore such things, and it was going to stand out too much. I wore cut-off jean shorts and Old Navy flip flops. I let my hair curl up all crazy in the humidity, and wadded it into a messy bun every day with a Goody's hair tie from Walmart. I wasn't a girl who got dolled up to meet a boy…or in this case, a man.

I'd considered not going at all, but then I looked in the mirror and saw what I'd made of myself. That other Teal that had suddenly started making all my decisions for me had done it again. I didn't know who that girl was that flat-ironed her hair for 45 minutes before leaving the house. But before I knew it, she was in that feminine little dress with freshly painted toenails—pink instead of blue—and wearing my skin to top it all off. I was worried she was slowly taking me over all together, and to be honest, I didn't really trust her too much. But, I left the house with her anyway.

I checked my phone for the time when the Crab Shack sign became visible. I'd given myself twenty minutes to make the walk from my house, but it had only taken me eleven. It was only 6:58 when the scent of the fried food seeped out of the building and up into my nostrils.

"Damn." I said out loud and checked my phone again, as if something would magically change the time.

There was nothing worse than looking too eager and showing up somewhere right on the money. I swear, it was even more embarrassing than being watched while vomiting. I considered walking around the block a time or two, forcing myself to be fashionably late, maybe rubbing the lipstick off while I was at it.

But then I spotted him, sitting on a bench outside the restaurant, waiting. He'd beaten me there. And he'd dressed too. He wore a white linen button down shirt, but the good kind, not some lame Tommy Bahama bullshit with the Hawaiian patterns on it. He had on long jeans, and some kind of leather flip flops, nicer than the ones you'd actually wear on the sand. His hair was almost combed neatly, definitely a lot better than it had been before. He'd shaved his face except for a little hint of shadowy scruff he'd left on purpose. He looked like a real person, a live one, about to meet a *woman*. And that was all it took to suddenly make me feel like one for the first time in my life.

I made my way over to him, almost sneakily, careful not to announce myself for some reason. I stood by him while he stared at his cracked iPhone for a few seconds before he looked up and saw me.

"Oh…hey. Where'd you come from?" He stood up and stuffed the phone into his pocket, a little bit twitchy. "You look nice tonight. I've not seen you all dressed up like that before."

"Oh…thanks." I almost scoffed, unable to accept a casual compliment, and then got a little twitchy myself. "I never have much of a reason to dress, spending most of my time doing Limeberry's grunt work, which always involves sand at some point." I glanced down at the dress. "I thought I'd take the opportunity, with dinner and all…and I could say the same about you. Looks like ya showered too." It actually smelled like it more than looked like it.

"Yeah. I haven't had a reason to dress in weeks. I got pretty grimy." He shrugged then looked at me like something new had just occurred to him. "I, uh, like your earrings. You design those?"

"Oh, yeah." I tugged at the gold-veneered shark's teeth a little. "I can't keep 'em though. I lent them to myself for the occasion this evening." I asked myself why in God's name I just revealed that to him, and could physically feel my cheeks getting redder by the second.

"I'm impressed." He said in the flattest and seemingly *unimpressed* voice.

I looked down at my shoes and kicked a pebble around on the sidewalk, unsure of what to say. But then, the weird silence announced itself. Strange how the quiet comes in as such an obnoxious guest. You expect it to just sit there doing nothing, but it moves like a ghost elephant through all the empty spaces between two people.

Will bent his knees and snap-clapped his hands together. "Well, um—shall we?" He reached past me and opened the door, the scent of crab legs and fried fish rushing us both with a big humid hug.

I said nothing and walked in while he held the door, too aware that he was watching me do it. It was such a small task, crossing a doorway, but it made me incredibly nervous. Or maybe it wasn't me that was really nervous. Maybe it was still that other girl who'd put my skin on without my permission. Maybe she was the one concerned about all the male/female date/non-date questions. It didn't seem like something I would have ever given a second thought to.

"How many?" The hostess smiled at us, and I immediately felt judged.

Was she wondering why I was here with the guy from the news? Or if she didn't recognize *him* (though she'd have to have been living under a rock), did she think I was here with my dad? No...no, he wasn't old enough to be my dad. Well, maybe if he was like one of those kids that slept with the teacher in eighth grade or something. He was old enough to be my dad in a way that would have led to a *20/20* special, but no, definitely not in a normal way.

"Two," Will answered, glancing at me out of the corner of his eye. I didn't know if I was standing still or fidgeting about like a mad woman, but my heart rate seemed to think I had progressed up to a brisk jog.

The girl showed us to a booth toward the back of the restaurant where we sat down across from one another. I immediately noted that it was the most hidden table in the restaurant, tucked in the back corner by the bathrooms, and couldn't help but wonder if she'd done it on purpose. Did she recognize Will? Was she frightened by him? Intrigued? I didn't know, but something told me that few things in life were ever accidents.

"Your server will be with you shortly," she said, setting down the menus and making no other pleasantries.

I smiled and nodded, then directed my attention to the laminated specials on the bright blue paper.

"Teal, are you all right? You seem a little...I don't know...like a little bit anxious or something." Will tried to make eye contact.

"Oh, no, fine." I shrugged. "I was just lookin' at the—the, um, surfboards hangin' on the walls. I've never noticed them before. There's always so many people in here, and so much goin' on. They're pretty cool though, huh? I forget to appreciate the beachy stuff, bein' from down here." I rambled mindlessly.

Will looked up at the multi-colored old surfboard and forced a smile. I immediately thought of how I shouldn't have brought up the beach. That's where his nightmare lived.

"I hear the she-crab soup is the best here," I said. "I think I might get it. I never get the touristy food; might be nice for once. Charleston is known for it, ya know. The she-crab." I tried something else, unable to find the ease from the last time we spoke.

"Look, Teal," his voice got quieter, "if you're embarrassed to be out with me because of, well, everything...the publicity and all, I get it. We can leave if you want to. I just thought maybe neither one of us should be alone right now. But if it's too mu—"

"Oh, no, Will. It isn't that. I'm sorry." I set down

the menu.

"You don't have to apologize—"

"I do, though. I *am* a little bit out of sorts, and I guess maybe it is that so much is goin' on right now. But you're right, I don't want to be alone in that empty house tonight. I need some sort of companionship with my little sidekick out of town. I'm happy to be here havin' dinner with you. Really. It's nice to have made a…a friend, I suppose." I was so confident when I said this, but my mind still floated the doubts from Smathers and my mother back in the darker corners.

"I appreciate that." Will smiled slightly then let his lips fade back to their natural melancholy state, like letting go of a stress relief ball. "Trust me. I know what it's like to miss your sidekick."

"*Oh, God.*" I closed my eyes and slowly reopened them. "I—I shouldn't have—" I fumbled for a moment, and tried to back out. But then, I thought, that's what everyone does when the subject of Chloe came up. So instead, I said something that surprised myself. "Do…you…want to talk about her? I wouldn't mind to hear about what she's like." I asked like I'd test the water on the first warm day of the year. One small part at a time.

"Nah…I didn't mean to bum you out right off the bat like that. Tonight is about trying to feel normal for a change, right? Sorry I'm already bringing the mood down." He rounded his shoulders into a smaller version of themselves.

"Maybe normal would be talkin' about what's important...not fakin' through it like you have to do all the time. You're not bringin' me down. Really." I shook my head as the waitress approached the table.

"Hi folks! Welcome to The Crab Shack. My name is Jen, and I'll be takin' care of y'all tonight. Can I start you off with somethin' to drink? An app maybe?"

"I'll just have water." I answered, also wondering if Jen had drawn the short straw.

"Yuengling....a tall boy, please." Will followed, his Boston accent thicker than ever.

"You got it," she answered him then looked back to me, her huge brown eyes beaming. "You sure you don't want a cocktail, hon?"

"No, thank you." I responded fast and awkwardly, causing Will to flash a half grin and shake his head, maybe wondering now what the hell *he* was doing there with me.

But when the waitress walked away, he seemed to breeze past it when he said, "She was born on the most perfect fall day New England had ever seen. The leaves were all bright orange by mid-October back in Massachusetts. It was as if they tried to shine their brightest for her that day. It was the top of the afternoon, the sun slicing in just right, 3:38 p.m. when she was born."

"I—I bet she was beautiful," I responded, my heart pounding in disbelief.

"She was such a great baby, too, hardly ever cried…perfect. Jessica got postpartum depression anyway. She couldn't even stand to hold her at the beginning. So I did the feedings and the changings, everything. We were best friends from the start, I guess."

I swallowed a big sip of water. "I'm glad she had…um, *has*…such a great dad. Great dads are hard to come by. It seems any dad is hard to come by for a lot of girls."

"I did my best," he said. "I try not to be so hard on Jess; I wanted a baby so much. Jess was bipolar. I didn't realize how severe it was. She had to stop the Lithium to get pregnant. We thought she was strong enough; she'd been so good for so long."

I nodded along, pretending to understand it more than I did. The only bipolar person I'd ever known was a girl from school who drew weird but impressive tattoos up and down her legs.

"I guess I shouldn't have pushed it so hard. She couldn't handle it. She tried. Chloe was nearly two when she finally took off. It was so sudden, but also had been a long time coming. Her old college roommate was living in Rome, and offered her a place to stay. And she went. Left us, just like that. She told me she was going. I believed her and didn't at the same time. She'd threatened so many times. But then, I picked Chloe up from daycare one day, brought her home, and found all of Jess' stuff gone."

"I'm so sorry, Will. I wish I knew somethin' to say. I can't imagine goin' through somethin' like that." I could feel both my sorrow and admiration for him growing all at the same time.

"It is what it is." He shrugged. "I wanted Chloe to have her mom, but I also knew Jess wasn't in a state to be one. She was sick of the meds, sick of the doctors, and sick of us, too, I guess. I eventually came to terms with it the best a person can...and I had Chloe, which was what was most important. Once Jess was gone, that's all that mattered. It's all I *let* matter."

"I get it. I never knew my dad; I mean, I don't even know who he is. And my mama is...I don't know what she is, really, but it isn't something that works all the way. I kind of like to compare her to an old car. I can get her started up most of the time, but knowin' full well that I might wind up on the side of the road in the rain, wonderin' what in the hell to do next. So, when Huckie came along, I got my best friend. He's only seven years old now, but he's my best thing in all the world. He's the thing that matters. He's like the purpose for my existence, I think. I can't imagine any other reason God would want me here. So I look out for him." I cocked my head and wondered what I'd have focused on without Huck. Combing the beaches looking for dead stuff probably wouldn't have been quite enough.

"That's how it was when I got my Chloe. I knew it was selfish of me, like I said. Maybe I wanted her because part of me could already feel Jess slipping away. She was so up and down…the most fun person you could ever meet, or the darkest, most depressed. It was exciting when we were just dating. She'd take off to the Cape at a moment's notice, or just strip down naked and dive into a creek on the side of a highway, completely unashamed of that beautiful body she had. Not a care in the world. It seemed so free at the time, like something I wished I could be. I wanted to, like, capture it in a jar, that energy she had. But then I realized that the power she had inside of her was what held her hostage. It would always turn into too much fun, then dwindle into just…despair. And I mean a despair most people never see, like catatonic, suicidal hell."

"It would be awful livin' like that…for both of you, I mean." I was now completely lost in everything he was telling me, almost *feeling* it, not just hearing it.

"I just tried to be there for her, not abandon her

whether she was staring at the damn wall that day or had decided to use our bill money to buy a designer bag. After we were married, though, when she'd take those downward spirals, she'd hate the sight of me...would hide away...never let me hold her. She was the one with the issues, and I felt so sorry for her. But I was alone. I thought maybe Chloe would perk her up, and the thought of a baby did. She had a great time picking out outfits and painting the nursery. We were happy. But once Chloe actually came, it was just never okay again. But I wasn't alone. It made it better for me, having someone in the house who loved me unconditionally, who wanted me to dry her tears, who came running as fast as she could when she heard my truck in the driveway. I felt guilty, but then I'd think maybe God himself sent her to me, meant to be. Then at the end of a beautiful sunny day by the water...he took her. And for what reason? Punishment, maybe? Now, without her...not knowing where she is..." He trailed off and his eyes glassed over.

I timidly uncurled my fingers that had remained clutched around my cheap purse strap while he spoke, and reached them toward his calloused hand that rested by the homemade salt shaker. I hesitated for only a second, but then committed. I cupped my hand over top of his and squeezed my palm around his warm fingers. He looked up and into my eyes and started to say something when the waitress sat the beer down with an obnoxious thud that scared me back to my side of the table. My water came next, and the moment was over. But for just a few seconds, neither of us felt alone anymore. Three fleeting moments of hot-blooded skin touching hot-blooded skin had been enough to help us both to breathe again, a pure, good breath, in and out.

CHAPTER 10

We trudged down Center Street with the sound of the waves getting fainter with each step we took toward the endless rows of cottages and beach bungalows. I could smell the uneaten hush puppies wafting out of my to go box, and was already thinking how good they'd be cold in the morning with Heinz-57 sauce on top. Cold leftovers were another secret joy in life. Almost as good as the window-unit air conditioners.

"Thanks for tonight." Will broke the silence and nudged my shoulder with his.

"For what? You wouldn't even let me pay for my own dinner." I nudged him back.

"For listening. I haven't felt comfortable enough with anyone to talk about Jessica…or Chloe. It's been me, by myself, trying to make some kind of sense of it all. But then you came along and made me feel a little less by myself for some reason. I know it got a little heavy in there, but I needed that. It's the first I've talked about all of this to anyone...well, other than the cops. And they're not exactly great listeners when you don't have the answers they want to hear."

"I know what you mean." I nodded. "I don't ever really feel like I know anybody enough to have a *real* talk about anything. And they damn sure don't know me. I just met you, but I feel like you're the first person I've ever actually known in this town. Well, except for Huck, of course."

"Yeah...but a seven-year-old can only offer you so much," said Will.

I raised my eyebrows and felt my cheeks warm.

"Uh, as for conversation, I mean." Will cracked a smile, though there was still a hint of sadness in it.

I swallowed hard and my heart bounced down low in my chest. "I didn't think you meant...I mean, I knew wh—"

"You know I'd give anything to have one more conversation with her about Paw Patrol," Will interrupted, "or Jean-Claire, who hogs the best books at school. You know that I'd kill to tell her one more spooky story like she loves."

"Yeah, I already miss Huck's chatter about this and that after he's only been gone for a day. I—" I stopped to die over what I'd said. I just kept doing that. "God, Will. I keep sayin' these things that I don't realize are horrible, it's just—"

"It's okay. You don't have to tiptoe around me, Teal. I know you have a brother her age. I know what we have in common here. You're not trying to twist the knife. You aren't saying anything wrong, but you are making me face it."

"That's not what I'm trying to do. I mean, I don't think it's my job or anythin' to get you to work through it."

"I know that, but it's what you're doing. I know it's more likely than not that my girl isn't—" He clenched his jaw.

"You don't have to—"

"No. No, dammit, I need to." He almost shouted. "I need to say it…out loud where I can hear it. That's the point. I'm glad you're making me face it. It's like you've been sent to make me do that in some way I can take it. You're like this *thing* that just rose up out of the ocean and made me look at all of this under the bright full moon. And you don't even know you're doing it."

I turned to face him directly. "Then say it. I'll be your witness." I let the runaway train go, knowing it needed to be set free, even if it crashed and burned.

"I know Chloe is most likely dead," he began, then swallowed hard, his voice only cracking a little bit. "She has probably been dead since the night she went missing on that beach. The evidence says she was kidnapped. The sand was a disheveled mess of tracks, and a shoe was left behind. She yelled, 'Catch me, Daddy,' then ran too far away for me to see her in the dark. Someone grabbed her, made her drop that sand bucket she loved, and spill her most prized shells everywhere. I know she probably died afraid and maybe even violated. I have imagined every sick fucking scenario, and I know what probably happened to her. I know I will long for her laugh, her voice, her fucking "No More Tears" shampoo. I will ache for it every day for the rest of my life. I know all of it."

I couldn't hold my own tears anymore and finally let one free to take the only journey it was bred for, down my rosy cheek, and then onto the ground.

"The thing is, Teal, maybe because of how close you are to Huck—or because of your feisty-ass spirit, I don't know—you make me feel nearer to her somehow. You make me feel connected to life the way she did when she came screaming into the world. I'd swear you'd met her or touched her, even."

"Will, I—" I took a step back from him, feeling that connection to her he knew I had, fully recognizing for maybe the first time that my life had brushed with hers, that it had been her on the beach that night.

"And if she is truly at *peace* somewhere now, I think she'd want me to have it too. And I swear to God I only feel like that's possible when you breeze through the alley I'm about to get drunk in, or the couch I've been passed out on. You make me want to get up and clean up for a few seconds of the day, and I don't know how in the hell you've done it so fast. You make me want to do something besides punching walls. Just breathe, maybe?" His voice was rushing in hard and wild on me, like the tide on a blood-moon night.

"Will…Will I think I need to tell you somethin'," I said. "It probably means nothin', but it might mean somethin'." I thought about the woman I saw on the beach the night Chloe went missing. I was letting myself realize that the girl I'd convinced myself had not been Chloe, *had* been. And after hearing all he'd just said, I couldn't hold it in any longer because I was too chicken-shit to get involved. Maybe she wasn't dead. Maybe whatever seemingly small thing I'd seen would mean *something* to someone, and she could still be found.

I was terrified, but I couldn't keep it in any longer. I had to say something because the dam inside of me was at its breaking point. It was time to get involved in the thing I'd sworn I wouldn't. I had to face the facts. I didn't know what was happening between me and the broken man I was with... but I owed him complete honesty. I might have very well been the last person to have seen his daughter before she became a missing person. That was the truth.

"I need to tell you that—" I took a deep breath.

"I think I know what you need to tell me." He grabbed me by the waist and pulled me close to his body. The to go box I'd been holding fell to the ground and busted around my feet. Then in one fluid motion his mouth was on mine, his delicious stubble highlighting the edges of his full, pouty lips. My hands went instinctively to the place where his jawline met his neck, and my teeth parted naturally letting him explore my mouth, passionately, hardly, but so much more skillfully than the few others who had been there first. Every part of my body reacted to him, pressed into him and wanted him. Everything else in my mind faded away. I didn't care what questions I should have asked him or what answers I should have given him. I only wanted all of him, and for him to have every bit of me. I was drunk, intoxicated, incapacitated by him. And I forgot about everything else.

CHAPTER 11

I woke up alone, in my own bed the next morning, the images from the night before reeling in my mind, torturing me. We'd somehow made it all the way back to the house across the street where Will probably still lay sleeping in his own bed. I wondered if he might, on off chance, be awake, staring at the ceiling, trying to make sense of how it all turned out the night before. I wondered if he, too, wished he could undo it all, make none of it matter, and go back to being the Teal and Will who just seemed to understand each other; just two people on the same wavelength, nothing else taken into consideration. I almost hoped that he couldn't sleep either, and that he couldn't get me out of his mind. I wanted him to be obsessing about how to fix it, and how to make me feel better. It was selfish. His daughter was missing, and I wanted to be taking up all of his brain space. I couldn't help it. Nothing could turn it off. And I started to hate myself for it, but couldn't turn my mind off enough to even do that right.

We'd stumbled in through the front door, pawing at each other, kissing frantically like they do in the movies. His mouth would move from my mouth to my neck, his hands running from my waist down to my hips, his scent covering my body and invading my chest. We'd collapsed to the couch that just days before he'd had his face so woefully buried into. But this time I'd fallen onto my back, his weight hovering over me, beating down on me like the sun on a perfectly hot summer day. I unbuttoned a few buttons on his shirt, and then he pulled it off over his head, unable to wait for me to get to the rest. My dress was already around my waist, and my legs wrapped around his hips. I could feel him, the part of him I was now starving for, grinding against me, leading me into a new part of my life that suddenly excited more than scared me. I imagined it's what it would feel like taking off in an airplane, terrified of something going wrong during the initial climb, but then getting to land in some new amazing place you'd wanted to see all of your life. There were a lot of things I'd never done.

I felt his hands move down my body and onto the waistband of my underwear. Had he just done it, had he just taken them off, I don't think I would have said anything. It would have just been happening; and I so badly wanted it to happen. But he wasn't in a hurry all of the sudden. He lingered for a moment, maybe to tease me, or maybe for permission, I didn't know...but that's when I said it. I uttered the simplest words—or maybe they're actually the most complex words ever—that changed everything.

"I just need ya know that I haven't done this before. I want to do it, but, I—I haven't yet. I felt like I should tell ya."

He stopped and looked into my eyes, completely out of breath. "Never?"

"*Never.*" I tried to whisper it like it was a good thing, leaning in to kiss him again.

"But you're...you're, um, eighteen right? I mean you're done with school, I know."

"I graduated back in May...I turn eighteen in September."

Will rose up and buried his face in his hands.

"What is it?" I asked out of breath.

"I'm so sorry, Teal. I got too...I was carried away. Everything we talked about tonight—I was feeling so emotional and close to you. I have such strong feelings for you....I do...I mean we *connected.* But....oh, God. We can't—" He looked me up and down...mortified.

I sat up and pulled my dress down over my thighs

that were still tingling from his weight.

"I'm so sorry…this is all my fault." He shook his head. "I'm vulnerable. God knows you are. You're vulnerable at seventeen even if you aren't vulnerable."

"Why are you sorry?" I whispered, rubbing my skinny arms with my hands.

"You're…you're an incredible person, Teal…but, you're not ready for this. You're fresh out of high school. You're a kid, for god sakes. I'm nearly *twenty years* older than you are. I could be your dad."

"If I'd been 18, you'd still have been old enough to be my dad. What difference does a little over a month make?" When I heard it, I realized I wasn't making the point that I had hoped to make.

"It isn't that," he said. "I wasn't thinking. We have this energy, and I'm just so damn…sad. I lost myself and almost robbed you of something that should be a really big deal…not something you give to a person you've only known for a few days. An amazing kid like you deserves a helluva lot better than a weepy old guy looking for some way to stop being so pathetic. That isn't enough for you, and someday you'll realize that and be thankful we stopped. And maybe you won't hate me for letting it get as far as it did."

I felt my cheeks burning from either

embarrassment or anger, maybe both. "I'm not a kid. I'm not pretendin' I'm some voluptuous full-grown woman suited to satisfy your every fantasy. But I'm not a kid. I haven't been a kid for a long time."

"You don't know what you are. That's the point," he answered.

"No, I don't know my ass from a hole in the ground right now. But neither do you. That's why it was fuckin' *magic* until you freaked out on me just now. I felt a little more like the thing I should be, would ever hope to be tonight, and so did you. The universe, the ocean, the moon, God...it all came together and made us *feel* life for the first time in who knows how long...maybe ever for me. My guess is that you've been sad for years, since Jess left, probably. And you know what? I've been miserable and alone my whole entire life. Forces of nature don't take age into any account. Maybe doin' somethin' to not feel sad anymore is a damn good reason to do it. I can't think of a better one."

"It was wrong—"

"Who decides wrong? My body is grown, and my soul needed to be close to someone else's. Yours damn sure did. I'm grown by the law that a bunch of suits made up in some dusty room somewhere *six weeks* from now. And I *know* you, Will. Dammit, I know your soul because whatever messed up gunk-washed-up-on-the beach shit it must look like under your skin is what mine looks like too. It doesn't matter that I've only known you for a few days. It only took a second for me to recognize that I *knew* you. I knew you before I even met you in some weird, past-life, alternate universe way. And don't you tell me it was any different for you because I'll know you're lyin' through your teeth."

He looked like he might speak for a second, but then he just stared at the floor instead. I gave him a good twenty seconds to say something to me to make me stay, but if he'd come up with it, it never made it out of his lips.

"I'm goin' home now," I huffed and stomped toward the door, trying to let the anger cover the embarrassment.

"Teal," he stood up and caught me by the arm.

"What?" I waited. "Say it now before you chicken out. What do you have for me behind that big wall, Will?"

He released his grasp on me. and his eyes fell to his cheeks. Then he stomped off into the back room and slammed the door behind him. The slam somehow played the music he'd written for it just perfect, music that sang relent more than it did anger. He was letting me go.

I went home and threw myself into bed…cried, then slept…peed, then cried, then slept again. Then I finally only slept. I convinced myself that everything always looked a little better in the morning, that all that the dark things in life needed was a bit of sunlight. But I found out what a lie that really was pretty fast when I opened my eyes. When the morning came, what had felt like a hurricane the night before now felt like that weird mega storm from *The Day After Tomorrow*. I couldn't imagine ever facing Will again. I was a whole lot angry at him, only the tiniest bit still afraid of him, but all of the way in love with him.

I glanced at my phone. 7:43 a.m. I was going to be late for work again. Bad late this time. I pulled myself up off of the mattress and headed for the shower. I bent down and turned the faucet on, tempering the icy water to a notch below scalding, and was just about to step in when the phone started vibrating on my nightstand. My wishful thinking told me it was Will, but my eyes read some unknown number with Surfside Beach, SC written underneath it.

"Hello?" I answered like I was already exasperated.

"Teal! Oh, my god." My mother shouted and whimpered. "Thank God you answered. I'm losin' my mind!"

"Mom? What in the world—"

"Teal…" She sobbed.

"What!? Tell me! What is it?" I screamed back.

"Why are you cryin'?"

"It's H...Huck," she croaked out. "Teal...Officer Smathers is comin' to get you and will bring you up here to me."

"Why!?" I shrieked. "What happened to Huck, Mama?"

"Oh God, Teal."

"What!? Get a hold of yourself and spit it out!" I yelled until my throat hurt.

"He's...he's gone!" She screamed into the phone, a gagging, shrill, vomit-inducing scream.

"Wh—where!? How!?" I begged in disbelief.

She wailed almost indecipherably. "We think somebody snatched him."

CHAPTER 12

I stared out of the window of the squad car, sobbing and chewing the skin around my nail beds until they looked like a bloody half-gnawed ribeye. One foot tapped and shook uncontrollably, but the rest of my body was numb as a day-old corpse. My fixed eyes watched a blur of palmetto trees racing by like the thoughts in my mind.

"We're almost there, Teal. Maybe ten minutes out." Officer Smathers threw his voice over the howling siren he'd just turned on, which somehow made everything even more real. "And, I know it'll be hard, but you should try your best to be easy on your mama. Be there for her. Don't blame her. The beach was crowded, and she'd only gone up to the concession stand to get him a hot dog. It could have happened to anybody. She's gonna need you more than ever."

I nodded and took another hunk of raw skin with my teeth.

"Ease up on your thumbs there," he said. "Gettin' an infection won't make this go away. We're gonna do everythin' we can, Teal. I know a lot of the guys at the department up there. Good ol' boys. They'll work with the feds well too. Just breath, one breath at a time. That's all you have to do right now."

"They're bringing in the feds?" I nodded to myself and spoke in an ironically calm tone of voice. "Makes sense."

Officer Smathers said nothing.

"They think Huck is connected with the others, don't they? The ring of abducted kids. He's one of them now, isn't he?"

"I can't really—"

"Don't give me that shit today! This is my brother. I'm a part of this!" I shouted like I never had before to someone I knew so little.

"I don't want to say somethin' I'm unsure about, or that would be unethical to say. Nor do I want to jeopardize the investigation. You have got to understand that, Teal. Do I know some things about a string of kidnappin's? Yes. Right now I don't know anythin' about what happened to your brother, though. Not until we get up there. Maybe he just ran off. It could be unrelated. It is a definite possibility.

When we get to the station I will look at the reports and talk to the officers. We'll go from there. We have no evidence at this moment that this is related to the others."

"But you don't believe that." I bit my lip and rolled my eyes.

Silence again.

"What if it is connected? Just prepare me. What do you guys think this is?" I paused, waiting for a response that didn't come. "Mama said she heard you talkin' to Limeberry the day y'all came in with Will. She said y'all might suspect human traffickin'. There any truth to that?"

"She heard me talkin' to Limeberry?" He sniffed in hard.

"She heard some. Enough. She heard those two key words that have scared us all to death. Now I want to know, could this be human traffickin'?"

Smathers let out a long sigh and adjusted his hat. "It…it is a possibility as well. But a lot of things are possibilities. That's why we don't want to start throwin' scary terms out to the public."

"Okay." I said as calmly as I could, letting it soak in while I watched the white dashes disappear, one after another, on the long road ahead of us. "What does that mean for Huck? What are we lookin' at here, really?"

"It means…it means it's gonna be hard."

"Oh, come on. No more B.S.," I said. "Please! I need the truth."

"The truth?" He hesitated. "It means that this thing is likely light years over South Carolina's head, and that we'll be workin' closely with the FBI from here on out. It means that the roots could go to other countries, drug cartels, sex traffickers, organ traffickers, child soldier recruiters, illicit adoption rings, or *anythin'* you might dream up and then some more. It means that we need to find the local connection...because there is one, and then we follow breadcrumbs. It means it's already a long shot, but we have to act fast. But it also means it's highly dangerous, and that you should keep out of it. I'll be your eyes and ears. All right?" He was nearly out of breath.

I couldn't respond. I had no words. I tried not to cry for a few seconds, but instead, to just take the medicine and think logically. I wanted to show Smathers that I could handle the information I'd begged him to tell me. So I just sat, holding my breath. It didn't work for long. Images I can't even repeat to myself flashed through my mind. I thought of every ugly and vile thing the world had to offer. Every movie scene, every bad picture from the internet, and every nightmare showed up for the party. I balled my fist and beat the pinky side of it against the glass. I screamed like a person normally would into a throw pillow, but there was nothing to muffle the sound of my concoction of frustration, fear and pure rage.

"Hey! Hey, you stop that. You'll break my damn window!" Smathers demanded before softening his tone a bit. "I—I know it's hard. And nothin' is gonna make it feel any better right now. Not even punchin' something'. When we get there, we'll get the facts, and we'll act *then*. We'll act with purpose in a way that matters. We aren't going to break glass just to look at all the sad pieces it leaves for us to clean up later. It won't make it better. It will only make a bad mess an even worse mess."

I heard what he said but not all the way. I didn't say anything back. I just fumbled in my cloth patchwork purse through gum wrappers and keys I'd never use until I got to my cell phone. I pulled it out and started scrolling frantically for Will's name.

"Who ya callin'?" Smathers asked.

"What's it to ya?" I snapped back.

"I just don't want ya talkin' too much about this until we know what it is we're talkin' about."

"It's all right. I'm just callin' Will. He deserves to know that it happened again, plus…I—I just want to tell him about it." I lowered my voice to a whisper.

"No." Officer Smathers tightened his hands on the wheel.

"What do ya mean, *no*?"

"No. Put the phone down. Now!" he shouted. "Have you been carryin' on with him any? I told ya to keep away and just do your job!"

"What's the problem? He needed a friend. I *needed* a friend."

"When is the last time ya saw him or spoke to him?"

"Last night. Why?" I could feel a number eleven forming between my eyes.

"Did he know where your mama and Huck went?"

"I—I think I mentioned they were gone somewhere to a Limeberry property in Surfside Beach yesterday mornin'. Why are ya askin' me all of these questions?"

"Dammit." Smathers stepped harder on the gas.

"What!?" I insisted. "Why are ya actin' this way?"

"Teal…Will Cianciola *is* a suspect, okay? The trouble has been and still is that all we've got is circumstantial…but it's bad. It won't hold up in court, but any idiot would put it all together."

"What are ya talkin' about? Tell me now." My voice matured from a kid's into an adult's in a matter of seconds.

"I'm a-tryin' to if you'd listen to me." The anger, or maybe it was worry, made Smathers trade his calm cop voice for one with a thicker, grittier accent.

"I didn't tell ya anything before because I can't go around accusin' people we haven't made an arrest on yet. But, looks like you're involved up to your ears now. The thing is…everywhere a youngin' has gone missin' is a place Cianciola has done a contractin' job for Limeberry Properties. Every single one of 'em. Because of that, he knows the coast of South Carolina like the back of his hand."

"But—but he was with me until really late last night. He doesn't even have a car with him in Folly…I don't think he could have rented a car or gotten a ride in the middle of the night and hauled ass to Surfside Beach. It doesn't even make any sense."

"No, but he coulda tipped somebody off. I told you, these things run deep. He knows the Limeberry properties outside of Charleston County better than you do. And you told him where a healthy prime-age boy with a vulnerable single mother would be all alone. I'm sure they had a tail on him all day yesterday and grabbed him at the one time Tracy looked away."

"But it couldn't be…I mean, the way he spoke about Chloe, and the pain he was in. It was so real and sad…it was, well, beautiful, in a messed up kind of way. Ya can't *fake* that."

"Ya tell any other person?" he went on.

"You. At the office."

"Anybody else?" He asked, more annoyed than ever.

I just stared at him.

"Didn't think so. It's Cianciola." He sped up to top speed. "Gotta be."

"Oh, my god." I brought my hand over my mouth to cover the gasp. "I just don't believe it. Just last night he was sayin' all of these soul-bearing things about the pain he's in, about how Chloe was his best friend in the world. He told me about how gorgeous it had been the day she was born, and how much he missed her. It was *real*."

"Spoke about her in the past tense, I bet. Like he knew she was gone for good?"

My face crumbled, and I darted my eyes around, hoping I'd see something in space to clear my confusion.

"People this high up the totem pole are very good, Teal. They create entire narratives that are so believable. They can make people feel anyway they want them to feel. And with feelin' comes believin'. It's just how it is. I wouldn't expect ya to be able to spot one of them. You're just a seventeen-year-old kid. I just wish you'd listened and stayed away from the bastard."

I started crying harder than I ever had. It was for my brother, for myself, for Chloe, and for things there weren't words for in the entire English language.

Then Smathers twisted the knife one more time. "If Will Cianciola *is* our pirate in the waters, then yesterday *you* gave him a treasure map to pure gold, girl."

CHAPTER 13

I expected the Surfside Beach police station to be buzzing with noise, ringing phones and running feet, but it was stormless. It was just like a regular day. I'd always thought that when huge cases like this one hit, that people began to shout and scramble around all over the place...and that maybe there'd even be some kind of mysterious theme music playing from some unknown source. More than assumed it, I expected there to be some sort of hustle and bustle. Didn't they realize that Huck McHone was someone's son and someone's brother? There should have been red-faced detectives with pit stains and loosened ties, screaming at rookie cops to do more. There should have been drawings on whiteboards and entire groups of officers gathered into small spaces, mapping out the search zones with protractors and No. 2 pencils. Perhaps there was somewhere, behind closed doors, maybe? But that's not the scene I walked into.

It was as though no one's little brother had gone missing at all, and perhaps they were all thinking about what they might have for dinner that evening. They could have been diligently working or scrolling through political memes, for all I knew. It was impossible to tell. A woman in a navy skirt and nude pantyhose carried a stack of files from one end of the room to the other. A receptionist wrote on something behind the desk. One guy with a badge walked around sipping a damn coffee from a Styrofoam cup. So normal. Not even an ominous look into the distance from anyone.

Officer Smathers handed me off to another officer. He told me his name because I could see his lips moving, but it definitely didn't make it all the way into my ear canal. Maybe that's what happened to all of the ado. Maybe everything *was* all stirred up, but it just wasn't making route all the way inside of me. Maybe it had been me who wasn't moving, wasn't hearing. Maybe in some sort of self-preservation I'd, in fact, shut off some of my senses. I hoped.

But I was able to see. So when the Surfside officer motioned for me, I blindly followed him into some kind of conference room where I first saw my mother. She was slumped into her own lap, her face buried into her hands, her body language speaking in some tongue I sure hadn't ever heard before. I could see the tears seeping through the cracks in between her ringed fingers, and falling onto her ripped jean shorts. Her posture was worse than it had been after Hank had been at her, the most lowdown I'd ever seen her.

"Mama," I reached out and stroked one of her bleached blonde curls.

"Teal!" She jumped up and wrapped her frail self around me. "Teal, oh, my god. You're here."

"I'm here, Mama. I'm not goin' anywhere."

I burst into tears, matching the force of hers while I breathed the nicotine out of her tank top and into my lungs. I had no words, not even the hint of any. So I just held onto her, sucking in her staleness, oddly comforted by its familiarity while the wetness from her face dampened the grooves of my neck.

Officer No Name spoke. "I'm so sorry for what you two are going through. But, if you'll have a seat now, we can go over a few things. I don't mean to pressure you, but time is of the essence." His voice was strong and commanded authority.

I released the embrace first, and we lowered ourselves onto the cracked pleather loveseat.

"Teal, I understand you are familiar with the Cianciola case that is currently under investigation back in Charleston County." The half-fat, middle-aged policeman looked at a file through his bifocal aviators.

"Yes," I nodded.

"Obviously, we think these two cases are connected, along with a few others along the South Carolina coastline. What can you tell me about the time you've spent with Will Cianciola?"

I swallowed hard. "Nothin' really. He—he's a screwed up man mournin' his missin' daughter. From what I've seen, anyway. I know Officer Smathers says he's a suspect, but I really—"

"Can you describe the time you spent with him? What was the nature of it?" He trudged on, all business.

"It was nothin', really." I answered quickly, glancing at my mother out of the side of my eye. "I got him settled into his cottage and chatted with him here and there. He's really only been around for a few days. That's all."

"Ms. McHone," he addressed my mother, "I'd like to ask you to excuse us for just a moment. Standard procedure."

"What do you need to say to her that you can't say in front of me?" She sniffled into a tissue.

Officer No Name nodded to a female officer outside of the door, who nodded back before coming in and taking my mother by the arm. "Let's go grab a coffee, hon. It's all right. This is just how they do things. You sure could use a little break, anyhow."

My mother shuffled out compliantly, though her face still protested when it looked back at me.

"Look, Teal, we have witnesses who have spotted you out with Will Cianciola. If there's something you didn't want to say in front of your mother, then say it to me now. Here's your chance. We know you were with him."

"So?" I said flatly.

"So, he's a suspect in these disappearances, and we need to find out what information you may or may not have."

"How...how is he a suspect? Because it's always got to be the father?" I repeated the thing he'd said to me the first night at the pier. "He loved Chloe...raised her on his own for cryin' out loud. She's all he has. His wife took off to Europe years ago and left them both alone. Chloe was all he had in the world."

"Maybe." The officer nodded.

"What do you mean, maybe? Does he have some other family I don't know about?"

"No, I mean, maybe his wife left him." He crossed his thick arms proudly.

"He told me that Jessica Cianciola left when Chloe was two years old," I stated with all the self-assurance in the world.

"No one has been able to locate the supposed ex-wife as of this moment. We have not confirmed her whereabouts. She's considered a missing person right now as well. Were you aware of that, Ms. McHone?" His smug voice grated me like a block of cheese.

I started to speak, but the space between the officer and my body swallowed up all the words.

"Are you ready to talk to me now?"

"I don't think I know anythin'." My eyes widened like a scared doe in front of a Mack truck.

"Come on, Teal. He cozied up to you and used you to get to your brother. Will you just answer my questions?"

"I—I'll try," I whispered, wrapping my arms around my body.

"When is the last time you saw Will Cianciola?"

"Last night. We—we had dinner at The Crab Shack on Folly Beach. Just because we didn't want to be by ourselves. It was nothin'."

"At any point in time did you disclose to him the location of your mother and brother?"

"No." I thought for a second. "Well, not then—it was earlier. I ran into him before work yesterday morning. I told him that Mom and Huck were at a Limeberry property in Surfside Beach, and then we made dinner plans."

"So you gave him the information, then didn't see him again for several hours? Is that correct?"

"Yes." I rolled my eyes.

"Okay. Teal, have you ever seen Will Cianciola converse or associate with Hank Feller?"

"*Hank?*" My eyes widened. "Of course not. I don't even think they know one another."

"No?" He faked surprise. "Even though they were both employed by Mr. Limeberry at the same locations and in similar time frames?"

"I never thought about it." My stomach started a gymnastics routine.

"Interesting. Isn't it though?" His smugness now jumped clear off his face and on to mine.

"What do you think?" I said. "That Will is somehow the brains behind traffickin' these kids, and that Hank is the muscle? You think they were just waitin' for the planets to line up so they could make it happen? You think Will told Hank where Mama and Huck would be and he rushed up and kidnapped my brother while I ate she-crab soup with the guy behind it? What's more…you think Will set up his own daughter's kidnappin'?" I'd found my way to my feet, though my swimming head told me to sit back down.

"We're just asking questions right now, Teal. I haven't mentioned any theories. You just did, though. Strange how a plausible scenario just jumped out at you so easily. Imagine, if you had the evidence to support it, how you'd feel."

"Do you?" I countered.

"Do I what?"

"Have evidence to support it?"

"I can't disclose what—"

"Yeah, yeah. Look, I don't know what's going on. But I don't think Will could possibly have had anything to do with this. Hank? Who knows? Somehow, maybe. I wouldn't put anythin' past Hank even though he has the IQ of a toddler. But not Will. There's someone else that could have—" I paused and swallowed hard. "I—I was on the beach the night Chloe Cianciola went missin'. I didn't think I saw anythin' at the time, honest, but maybe…maybe I did. And it wasn't Hank or Will."

"What are you talking about?" He leaned onto his elbows.

"There was this wom—"

"Detective, can I see you for a moment, please?" A deep voice sliced into the room, and an officer I hadn't met yet trudged through the door.

"Can you give us just a second? I'm wrapping up with Teal here." *Detective* No Name, as it were, responded.

"I'm afraid this can't wait. It's urgent regarding our abduction cases." His face was like packed sand. Strong, vast, blank.

Detective No Name glanced at me to say, *Don't go anywhere. I'll just be a second.*

I said nothing in return, just folded my arms, fully aware that I didn't have much of a choice in the matter.

I could hear his muffled whispers to the other officer who'd pulled him out. I couldn't quite make out what they were saying, but No Name didn't sound pleased from the huffing, moaning and chubby arms thrown into the air. I stretched my knock-off Converse tennis shoe out toward the door, and slid myself, chair and all, closer to it so that I could hear them better.

"Well, there go a couple theories," No Name said, rubbing his temples before adding, "and now a couple of bodies on our hands and fragile people to notify about the situation. If this wasn't a mess already, it sure as shit is now. I don't know where we even go from here."

"I know. What do you want me to do, Detective?" The other, obviously low-in-the-ranks officer asked him.

"I'll finish up with the girl in here. See what else she has to tell us before we reveal anything to her. You go break the news to Tracy McHone. Take some tissues with you. This ain't gonna be easy on her."

CHAPTER 14

"I'm sorry about that, Teal. Now, where were we?" The detective sat down casually when he reentered the boxy room.

"What was all that about out there?" Did he *not* think I could overhear parts of it?

"That's...never mind that. You were about to tell me about something you saw on the beach the night Chloe Cianciola went missing. Can you state the date of that night, please?"

"I'm not tellin' you shit until you tell me what's goin' on!" I demanded.

"You're speaking to an officer of the law, young lady. Need I remind you?" He eased back into his chair so casual-like, and it itched like poison oak at my already-irritated skin. And as cracked open and oozing as I already felt, I was liable to tear up the next things that so much as brushed by me. He was getting far too close.

"You said you have bodies on your hands and fragile people to notify. Includin' my mother. Now, who died?" I never broke my gaze into his eyes that reminded me of the polluted swamp water by the paper mill across town.

"Teal, I'm afraid I can't—"

"Who!? Was one of them my brother? Tell me now, dammit! Did you find my little brother somewhere?" I screamed, slinging spit and snot across the room.

"Teal..."

"Tell me!"

"No Teal, it was not your brother. We have not located the whereabouts of your brother. Now please, please calm down."

"Then...who? Who was it?" I asked more calmly, lowering myself to my chair. "Chloe?"

"We haven't notified the next of kin yet. When we do, then I can release that information. But I will not disclose it to you under any circumstances."

"But one of the people you had to notify was my mother. If she's next of kin, then so am I."

"It doesn't work like that. I'll let her tell you if she chooses. I'll tell you though, it isn't a family member of yours...just someone who didn't have anybody else. Okay?"

I exhaled deeply, knowing I'd lost this particular

battle. "Well, are we done here, then? I need to go be with my mother. Apparently she's gettin' some really bad news right about now."

"Almost. What did you see at the beach the night Chloe Cianciola went missing? The faster you tell me that, the faster we can move on from this."

I rolled my eyes and let out a sigh. "Sorry, I got distracted with the talk of dead bodies showin' up everywhere."

"Ms. McHone..." He drew my name out, a clear reprimand.

"I was down there by myself, just collectin' shells and shark's teeth, like I always do," I began. "I was near the pier, maybe fifty yards away from it, about to turn around and go back home. I saw a woman draggin' a child away by the elbow, like a kid pitchin' a fit at the supermarket or somethin'. It didn't seem all that out of place until later when Huck started babblin' on about a woman that would come up to kids at the beach and invite them to some kind of day camp."

"All right." He nodded along as he jotted on his notepad.

"I can't really remember what the kid had on, but the description matches Chloe's. Age, height, hair color...all of it. I—I tried to put it out of my head. I thought maybe I was wrong, that it wasn't Chloe, and I'd just embarass myself by bringin' it up. I thought a bratty kid just didn't want to leave the beach. But now I think—maybe...I don't know. Somethin' Huck said just rang a bell, and I got to thinkin' on it...I think I could have seen—" I shook my head.

"Maybe you saw the kidnapper." He finished my sentence.

"I—I wouldn't say—"

"What did the woman with her look like? Everything. Age, hair, eyes, build, freckles and moles. Everything about her."

"Um...she looked like she was a mama's age. Like late thirties, maybe. I couldn't see her eyes. I think her hair was shoulder length and blondish, but like it might be darker in the wintertime. You know the kind. She was average height, like five-four or five-five. Average build. That's all I can really remember. She looked so *normal*. She was definitely someone who probably goes unnoticed most places. Nothing particularly bad or good about her."

"Okay. Here's what we're gonna do, Teal. I'm gonna send you to the sketch artist. In the meantime you try to focus your mind on the face that you saw. Think of the expression, curve of the jawline, if she grinned at you, if she had dimples, where fine lines were showing up...every little thing you can. Okay?"

"Okay." I nodded.

"So, um, do you think maybe this could mean that this doesn't have anythin' to do with Will, or Hank Feller, even?"

The officer took a deep breath in and out, and then replied, "Why don't we go talk to your mama now."

CHAPTER 15

The detective led me into a smaller and quieter room that had a vase full of lilies perfuming it from some sort of second-hand end table. The urns of flowers almost covered all of the scratches and coffee rings all over it, but not quite. There was also a pastel rug in the floor meant to distract us from the drab beige couch. I supposed this was the room people were sent to get the bad news, like somehow a couple flowers and sparse bits of color awkwardly thrown around would help. I hated it right off the bat. It was my opinion that bad news should be delivered in an ugly place, like outback by the reeking dumpsters.

Smells always conjured up memories for me. I wouldn't have wanted to be happily trotting along in a garden somewhere and then be transported back to something awful because the perennials were blooming again. I didn't want to associate the good with the bad, and get them all mixed up together like that. It would be like throwing a pair of red panties in with all your white clothes…it'd just spill onto everything else and ruin it. I say keep the bad with bad, and the good with the good, but that's just me.

Mama didn't seem to notice any of it or anything else, for that matter. She wasn't crying when I walked in the room, but it looked like she had been. She was just sitting there, staring into space with a box of tissues resting on her lap. Her eyes weren't really focused on anything in particular, and her whole body was sort of limp. I think if I'd barely poked her, she would have just toppled over.

"What is it, Mama?" I lowered myself into a squatted position next to her, resting my hand on her knobby knee, careful to keep it centered and steady.

"I—I can't believe it. With everything else…now this." She shook her head slowly and looked to the side like someone was there, and the sun highlighted her face in such a way that I could see how she used to be pretty.

"What, Mama? Tell me." I whispered, my own stomach dropping.

"It—it's Hank." She looked me in the face, hers still relatively blank. "Hank's dead, Teal."

"What?" My eyes widened, mostly out of shock…and maybe a tiny twinge of sadness. I'd hated Hank as close as I could get to hating anybody. But, isn't there always a sort of sadness when anybody dies? Especially if they die without redemption…just die in the middle of the mess they'd made of their life? I always thought so.

"They found him slumped over in his truck," she began. "They said there were empty liquor bottles everywhere. He was parked back in one of the coves, off-road, up near Morris Island Lighthouse. Drank himself to death. The cop said he'd been dead for a couple days when they got to him. He probably died right there the night we fought. Smathers had been lookin' for him. After he stormed out of the house he went down to some bar and started in on everybody. Knocked a boy out. Then he left. Looks like he drove straight to that cove then, and kept goin' till it got him this time." She trailed off into a whisper and stared into the stale air around us, looking for something or somebody. I didn't know what, and my guess was that she didn't know either. Then she added, "If I hadn't left that night and had gone lookin' for him, he might still be alive. He'd be alive, and Huck wouldn't be missin'."

"I'm—I'm so sorry, Mama. I know that despite everythin', you cared about Hank a lot. And I know you love Huck. But you can't blame yourself. There isn't time for it. I know you're in a lot of pain right now. What can I do to help you?" My mouth said these comforting words to her, but my mind raced with a thousand other things. For instance, if Hank had died that night, there's no way he knew where Mama and Huck went. So there was no way he was involved in all of this. Did that make Will look more or less suspicious now? I didn't know. I tried to shake it out of my head and just be there for my mother. "Talk to me, Mama. What can I do?" I tried again.

She shrugged and smiled one of those crooked 'to hell with it' grins, and I tried to direct my mind to keep doing as it had been told. I knew that a person always had to try to offer help to someone in grief because it was just the right thing to do. But I also knew good and well that there wasn't a damn thing in the world I could have ever hoped to do to make it any better. Grief just had to run its course like a bad virus. Once the fever spiked, and you'd puked down to your yellow and bitter stomach lining, it'd be over, but not a minute before. You could pray to the Good Lord above to let it be the last time you'd get that familiar dizzy nausea and start heaving again, but it wouldn't matter. It would never stop till it decided to stop. Not an antibiotic on God's wild green planet could ever change it. But finally you'd be empty again, and then you could start to heal. Mama was just starting the journey, and I knew it would be a long night of holding her hair back.

"Well, I'm here, Mama. I'm gonna do everythin' I can to help bring Huck home. That's what I can try to do right now. That's what we *can* still change, and it's what we should focus on. Okay?"

She rolled her lips in toward her teeth and nodded. I put my arms around her and lowered her tired head onto my chest. I could feel my shirt getting damp immediately, and I said, "Just cry it all out. Every bit, till it's all gone." Then I rocked her like a baby. That's all I knew to do.

"Teal," the detective's voice sliced in sideways from where he stood half in the doorway. "I'm sorry to interrupt you two, but the sketch artist is ready for you now. We don't have any time to lose. I need you to come on with me now. I'll get someone to come sit with your mama."

I nodded and carefully picked my mother's head up off of my chest with my hands. I kissed her on the forehead, and smoothed her sweaty hair back from her eyes. "I'll be back in just a minute, okay?"

She nodded, eyes bloodshot, her mind still darting about the room.

"Okay," I stood up and followed the detective back onto the tiled floor and into the normal hallway that had no flowers to offset all the ugly.

"Our sketch artist is really good. You just tell him everything, down to the thickness of her hair, the size of her pores. Everything, all right?"

"All right." I nodded, trailing behind him like a short-legged dog struggling to keep up with his master.

We made our way back into the main room, the one with desks everywhere and not enough clamor to suit me. The detective turned toward an office where I saw another man setting up an easel, but my eyes focused elsewhere. The disheveled dark hair I'd only known for days, but knew so well at the same time, rounded the corner across the room from us. His back was to me as he followed the uniform in front of him. I looked toward the sketch artist, then shifted back to where Will walked so somberly. I quietly fell out of line and slow-jogged across the station floor until I was so close to him that I could smell his scent...whatever it was. Ocean. Sweat. Degree deodorant.

"Will." I reached out and touched his arm, sort of out of breath for a reason that didn't make any sense to me.

He turned around and eyed me. "What do you want?" he snapped in a hushed but hateful tone.

"Um....I—" I stumbled over my words shocked at his callousness.

"I have more *questioning* to get to. So what is it you need, Teal?" He flared his nostrils out wide, like the lizard that lived on my front porch did when I got too close to him. And also like Will, he'd change colors fast.

"Why are you bein' like this?" I questioned him with the face of a scolded puppy.

"Oh...I don't know. Maybe it's because, according to the officer that called me in here, 'that little neighbor girl of mine saw a woman on the beach with Chloe that night.' So they are about to identify my *accomplice*." He flashed air quotes and clenched his jaw before adding, "Why in the hell didn't you tell me or the police that you saw somebody that night? Forget that they still think I had something to do with this. They could have found her, Teal! So much time has been wasted because of you! Why'd you sit on it? So you could come play house with me, little girl? Do you have any idea what you might have done here!?" he screamed as the tears shot out of my eyes.

"Hey!" The detective realized that he'd lost his tail and came running toward us about the time the officer who Will had been following grabbed his arms to pull him back.

"I—I didn't mean to. I thought it was nothin'...I didn't want to be wrong. I—" I sobbed and stumbled as a set of hands grabbed me too.

"Well, it turns out it was something." He struggled.

"Maybe it was just Jessica, trying to get her

back…maybe someone who wouldn't hurt her, maybe—"

"Well, they also called me up here to tell me that Jessica's dead. Killed herself over a year ago in Italy. They finally got a hold of a death certificate, sent over from some little town on the Mediterranean. So there goes that theory, Special Agent McHone. She's dead, and maybe Chloe, too. Thanks for your help!" he shouted as they pulled him into a room and shut the door.

"Oh, my god. *Jessica* wasn't the other person? I thought…\'I'm so sorry—" I stopped trying, knowing he could no longer hear me.

"Come on now, Teal. We've got work to do." The detective redirected my suddenly limp yet compliant body toward the room where the sketch artist was all set up and waiting. "Time to make things as right as you can now, sweetheart."

PART 2

TRACY

CHAPTER 16

It was quiet back at the townhouse Limeberry had put us up in. And I hated too much quiet—it was eerie—I mean, think about it. Where are we asked to hush our mouths? Funerals, graveyards, libraries...Libraries are the worst of them all; dust everywhere, women born in 1846 named Thelma, who smell like moth balls and formaldehyde running the joint. God, I hated libraries, but not as much as I'd hated sitting at that police station all day long. I couldn't have taken one more second of sitting in that odd-looking room where the sun burnt me through the window like an ant beneath a magnifying glass, waiting on Teal to finish up with that sketch artist. I wasn't glad one ounce to be where I was at another Limeberry setup now, but then, I guess I was glad to be anywhere but that little room. I never wanted to go back to the little room.

I grabbed my half-gone pack of Newport menthols and the full bottle of Old Crow and eased out of the squawking door and onto the front porch as quietly as I could. Teal had finally cried herself to sleep on the couch watching some old rerun of "Friends." It was the one where they made all those New Year's resolutions, and Ross couldn't get his new leather britches back up. It was weird watching it play out in the background of my messed up life, listening to that '90s laugh track. I swear, it felt like the audience was laughing at us, me and Teal.

She'd had a day almost as bad as mine at the police station. Spending nearly three hours getting grilled by a skinny guy with a superiority complex and a piece of charcoal about the looks of a woman she saw for two seconds at dusk once hadn't been any day at the beach for her either. I hated seeing her this way more than anything. She should have been down on the shoreline digging for those nasty-ass bones she likes so much. I'd always wished that anything could make me as happy as unearthing dead things on the beach made Teal. It was hard to see her so emptied of her spunk, like watching a popped balloon falling back to the ground. That spunk of hers was what kept me going most days. I'd just feed off her energy like a sedan catching speed off tailgating a semi on the highway. I reckoned pure exhaustion had finally set in, though. A person could only fight it so long before the body'd shut it all down. I was kind of looking forward to it happening for me. Hell, I was waiting for it like a hot date who's an hour late.

I'd always thought of myself as tough as nails, even though everybody else thought I was a flimsy wet noodle of a person, especially Teal. But nothing would ever break me. It didn't break me when my daddy would come home drunk from his shitty shrimp boating job just sober enough to still knock me and my sisters around. It didn't break me when Teal's daddy knocked me up during his Spring Break to the beach then went back to the upstate and refused to take my calls. It didn't break me when Huck's daddy, who'd promised to marry me, begged me for an abortion instead. And I wasn't going to break now. Hank Feller sure as hell wasn't going to be the one to do it. Yeah, he'd gotten a few of my tears, a couple handfuls of my hair, and way too much of my time…but much less of my heart than anybody would think. He just warmed a cold spot on the bed next to me on lonely nights. Nobody ever wanted to sleep on cold sheets. It's why I let the cheap, Walmart-variety space-heaters-for-men into my room at all. Some of them were good, and most of them were bad, but none of them mattered enough to dissolve me. Once one would crap out, another was plenty easy to come by. But this thing with

Huck; it was different. It could have melted steel.

I sat on a half-rusted metal chair and hoped for lightning when I lit the first cigarette of the chain I'd planned on smoking for the evening. Limeberry had put us up in Surfside just like he did Cianciola back in Folly. His Horry County version of me, some overly excited woman named Karen, had gotten me all settled before Teal had even made it up the coastline. It would have been nice to have had her with me when it all went down. She was always so good at letting people lean on her. Sometimes it felt like I relied on her more than she relied on me. I was okay at keeping up with myself, but I never learned how to be a crutch for somebody else. And everyone needed a crutch every now and then, especially children. Somehow Teal saw that I couldn't be it, and became it for all of us. I was happy for just a minute when I saw that much better version of my face bounding into the police station. For a minute she'd made it okay by just being there; such a tough little thing she always was.

Before she showed up I'd felt as awkward as a mama's boy at a gala in a blue tuxedo for a lot of reasons. First of all, I had been alone, and second of all, I was now on the other side of everything we'd just been through with Cianciola. When Karen came to let me into the charity housing I was to stay in while my kid was gone, I hit rock bottom. I hated getting waited on, felt *sorry* for. I might as well have signed my last bits of pride away with pen and paper. I cracked. I was no better than that sad sack man who'd stood in the office a few days before. I was the new Cianciola.

It seemed like the Limeberry properties had become some sort of looney bin housing for the parents of missing children, and now I was suddenly a tenant. This time it was a little row of townhouses. They were much newer and nicer than what we had back in Folly. I didn't know if I was grateful for that, or if it made me realize what a cheap son of a bitch my boss had been for making me live in something one notch above a shack for all those years. He obviously wasn't hurting for money. The place was fine, but it still felt like checking into that hotel from "The Shining." I just knew I was a part of something bad, stuck in a place meant for agony.

I took in a long drag off the cigarette while I scowled on purpose and thought on it some more. I wanted to be in the bad mood I was in. I wanted to be mad—mad at anything in the world I could pass to be mad at. It didn't matter what it was. But I didn't want to think about Huck. It burned too much from the inside out…like getting skewered like a hog and then slow-cooked to death. The truth was—in some part of my body I couldn't feel—I didn't believe I'd see him again.

I'd sucked my one happy little vice down until I'd made a stump out of it. It was so short that I could feel the heat from the root of it on my fingers when the car pulled up, some Honda with an Uber sticker on it. Will Cianciola appeared out of the back passenger side door and walked toward the unit a couple doors down from mine and Teal's. I took my last draw while I stared at him as he walked, and I followed him with my narrowed eyes all the way to the stoop. I watched him stick the key in the door and open it up. And then he'd almost walked in, but turned around to look at me instead. Maybe my gaze spit fire like a dragon, and he'd felt it land on him.

"Is there something I can do for you?" he asked, exasperated from the start.

"I guess Limeberry put you up too," I croaked back. "I didn't realize that the housin' was for suspects as well. I figured they'd-a held you in the slammer. What, not enough to hold ya yet?"

He didn't say anything back, just started through his threshold again.

"Don't just run off when someone is talkin' to ya now, Yankee. Don't you know that's considered awful rude down here?" I called out to goad him, waving the Old Crow bottle around, not noticing what little liquid was left in it, my hips swaying in an awkward dance.

"What?" He slammed down his faded leather

overnight bag. "What would you like me to say to you, Tracy? You obviously have a pretty damned strong opinion about me already."

I pulled a second cigarette out of the pack and eyed him good.

"I don't have time for this," he huffed and tried to walk off again.

"You have anything to do with my boy bein' gone?" I shouted out as strongly as I could, but heard my voice crack toward the end. "Just look me in the eye and answer me. I gotta know. Did you take him?"

"No," he answered flatly, the dark color of his eyes pouring into mine.

"Any idea who did?" I asked sternly, never breaking the gaze.

"No." Still solid as a rock.

I just stared at him.

"But I know that's not good enough," he finally said. "It's not good enough for the cops or for anybody else. And no, they didn't have enough to hold me, because there's nothing there. I feel like my guts are being ripped out on the operating table while I'm under some kind of anesthesia that keeps me from moving, but I can still feel it all. I'm screaming and no one can hear me. And I'm alone. And it's fucking hell. What else you got?" He threw his hands down by his side, and then added a little more softly,

"My child is missing, too, and I'm not even afforded the opportunity to grieve over it. How would you feel if they were doing you this way right now?"

I stood up and exhaled the smoke as I walked toward him. There were two other pretty pastel stoops separating mine from his, but I could see him good. I looked him square in the eyes, so hard that I wondered if some of the blue off mine would seep right into his and speckle them into marbles. And I believed him. I don't know why or how, but I absolutely believed him from the tips of my red toes to the top of my bleached out head. He didn't know anything about his daughter or about my son.

"I got half a bottle of cheap whiskey." I picked up the glass jug and shook it. "You want some?"

He didn't speak back, but instead just shot me a look that said he'd given up. Then he turned to walk into his assigned unit and left his door wide-ass open, deliberate as could be, to motion for me to come right on over.

CHAPTER 17

I peered in through the window on Teal to make sure that she was still sleeping soundly on the couch, then I took the bait. I wiggled my bare feet into a pair of old rubber flip flops, and made my way across the two little neatly manicured mini yards in between Will's sad shack and mine. I don't know what in hell I hoped to achieve by taking my little field trip, but I supposed that the alcohol would help me out with that. All I knew was that sitting alone in silence would be torture; I'd never been great at solitude.

I didn't knock when I got over there, and he didn't greet me when I came traipsing in either. Nobody was in the mood for any kind of small talk. We were in the mood to drink and stay quiet, just lonely enough to want to hear another person breathe somewhere nearby, but not much more. We didn't expect comfort or laughs. We just expected to sit beside another miserable person and swallow the brownish liquid until we felt numb. Maybe another body nearby would just warm up all the things that made us feel cold square on the height of a South Carolina summer.

Two shots came and went within just a minute or two of me stepping my tattooed foot through the front door. We stared at each other in complete silence for a while before taking the third. But by that fourth one, we were giggling through half-sad, half-bent tears, sloshing the best medicine on the market out of the spotted shot glasses. Will had already pulled them out of the cabinet by the time I walked in. I knew they'd be there ready for me too. No Limeberry property was complete without a cabinet full of bar glasses, including the ones for shots…maybe the most important of them all. The shortest and the most plain of all the glasses, the ones that wore their purposes in their little statures, were our saving graces. The tiniest of all the cups had the unique talent to soar like military missiles, always landing with perfect precision straight on the target. They by-God got the job done. They got you drunk, and people at the beach always wanted to be drunk. Happy or sad.

Even though we eventually laughed (at what, I don't know) and looked back and forth at one another, we didn't talk much. It might not have been at all if I really think about it. It was hard to recall. Except for one thing I said that still hurts like a cluster headache when I think about it. I remember it because it might have been the only thing I had said at all, and I knew it was damn-well true too.

Will had stumbled over to the outdated radio, one of the kinds with the dials and antennae and everything, and flipped it on. I supposed he needed something to crawl into the air and ease up the tension, because it certainly wasn't going to be any kind of human connection with me. There wasn't any. We were more like two seashells left beside each other on the sand. Just there—no personality, no goals and no hope, too chipped for anyone to want. We were just little pieces of matter taking up space in the world; whatever living thing that had once been inside, long gone. But sometimes music could work on an awkward situation like BENGAY on a sore knee. It would seep in, warm it up, distract you from the stiffness, and then numb the areas that throbbed enough for a minute or two of relief. It wouldn't fix anything, really, but it could chase the sting away for some small period of time.

I was relieved to hear the first few notes seep out of the outdated piece of junk myself. I heard the familiar old tune, ba-da-ba-bump, ba-da-ba-bump. Then the lyrics. *When your baby leaves you all* *alone\ And nobody call you on the phone\ Doncha feel like cryin'\ Doncha feel like cryin'\ Well, here I am, my honey c'mon baby, cry to me.*

"Dirty Dancing. The scene in Johnny's cabin after Penny's botched abortion..." Will chuckled and pointed to the radio. "It was Jess' favorite movie. She made me curl up on the couch and watch it with her on our third date, then a million more times. Perfect." He hurriedly took another swig. "Fucking perfect."

The song carried on. *When you're all alone in your lonely room\ And there's nothing but the smell of her perfume.* I listened to the melody, swaying back and forth a little bit, and let myself remember when I'd first seen the movie myself. I'd vowed then and there, barely out of my feety pajamas that I'd marry Patrick Swayze...either him or Donnie from New Kids On The Block. I'm glad I didn't know then what a far cry from being the wife to a gorgeous movie-star my life would actually turn out to be. You need hope like that as a kid, that maybe it'll all turn out all right. But still, even though my life didn't pan out, the song did do something for me. It changed me from a lifeless shell to just a sorry excuse for a breathing human again. Music will do it every time. Just like the BENGAY.

I walked toward Will, standing up out of my lonely corner, my thighs pulling up off the slick chair like tape. He looked up at me, two expressions for the price of one. He had some level of both disgust and just plain ol' giving up on his sweaty, humid face. It wasn't because I was unattractive for my age, even though I smelled like alcohol and cigarettes…not just from tonight, but set-in alcohol and cigarettes. It was because of the fact that he didn't even like me, and felt like a homeless man about to dumpster dive for a half-eaten hamburger. He'd get fed, but had resorted to stooping to getting whatever he could just to survive for another night. And, hey, I was right there too. I was the next homeless, penniless hobo in line, hoping for a scrap or two out of that pile myself. Finally, something we had in common.

He leaned in, reeking of drinking too much whiskey and wearing the same sweat-soaked shirt for at least a day. And I met him with dried out lips and a whisper of smoke still doing a fire dance on my tonsils. We kissed for a minute, an angry, wet, bad-tasting one, just because we had to start somewhere. Then he left my mouth, and went straight for my worn-out blue jean shorts…well actually they were a pair of Teal's that were a whole size too small for me that I'd shoved into my overnight bag the night I left Folly.

"I'm a piss poor mother." I croaked out as he lowered to his knees to try to shimmy the skin-tight denim down over my narrow, but not narrow enough, hips. And that's the one thing I could remember saying. The true thing that I spoke out loud was that I was a terrible, terrible mother.

"I was a good father...I was..." He mumbled as he finally got the shorts low enough for me to step out of them.

When he pulled me to the floor by the fridge, I felt my bare ass stick to the gritty 1980s linoleum underneath me. I knew there'd be nothing to get me ready, because this wasn't about that. It wasn't about pleasure or tenderness. It wasn't even about wanting. It was about trying to get to the end game to either feel a little better, or a little worse for a second, and I didn't know which one it was. It was gonna burn and struggle... how I think we both needed it to feel because of that ache in the part of our brains that the absence of our kids had damaged forever in that first frantic second that we knew they were really gone. The song kept pumping into my ears as he pumped gruffly into me. *Nothing could be sadder than a glass of wine alone\ Loneliness, loneliness, it's just a waste of your time.*

I stared at the ceiling for most of it. I was either embarrassed to look at him, or just wanted to avoid anything that could possibly wind up in a real connection. I didn't know. But when he sped up and his muscles tried to claw out of his shiny, damp arms, I looked at him for a split second. I looked at him just long enough to see the tear fall out of his eye. I thought, at first, it had been a drop of sweat, but no, it was a bona fide tear. Then I felt it land on my shirt and seep through to my chest. And when it did, it triggered a sting in my own distant eye. The final lyrics bellowed out with the two of us now rocking into a different kind of embrace that matched the tortured melody. *When you're waiting for a voice to come\ In the night there is\ no one\ Doncha feel like cryin'\ Doncha feel like cr-cr-cr-cr-cr-cr-cryin\ Cry to me.*

CHAPTER 18

The sun had just come up when I stumbled through the creaking door of our Limeberry-assigned townhouse. I tried to ease in as quietly as I could, careful not to wake Teal. However, when I turned the lamp on, I found her sitting up on the couch. She was wide awake, and as straight as an arrow, like her back was taped to a flagpole. Her hands were resting gently on her skinny thighs that were at a perfect ninety degree angle with the floor. Her eyes were the spookiest part, fixed straight ahead like the corpse of a woman who had died with her eyes wide open. Her jaw was clenched, but not enough to make her look anything but even more scary-still. It was like she'd banished the 'Teal' out of her body, and I was looking at the shell she had shed and left behind. It was kind of like stepping on a rattlesnake skin in the woods, and honestly, it scared the hell out of me.

"Teal," I said monotone but loud, like speaking to an old lady hard of hearing.

Nothing.

"Teal McHone." I waved a hand in front of her face. "Anybody home, honey? What's wrong with you? Why are you up? Did somethin' happen? Did the police call or somethin'? Is it about Huck?" My heart tried to claw out of my sun-spotted chest.

She turned her head, stiff-necked like a robot, toward me. "Where were you?"

"I went out for a minute. What's up with you? You're really scarin' me." I held my hand over my heart like I was getting ready to say the Pledge of Allegiance.

"I saw you out the window when I woke up. *Last night.* You went into that unit a couple doors down from here. I logged into the Limeberry database from my phone to see whose it was. It says that's where they put Will up. Were you over there with him for some reason?" She still showed no emotion.

"Yeah, honey…I—I saw him go in. I just went over to talk to him for a minute. I—I know he's a suspect, and that might seem weird to you that I'd be over there. Wait, have you been sittin' up like this all ni—"

"Why do you look like that?" She cut me off.

"Like what?" I asked as doe-eyed as I could

while I tried to smooth my hair down a little bit. That probably only hurt my case.

"Like *that*." She lifted a limp arm toward me. "Your clothes are all wrinkled. Your hair is flat in the back. Your makeup is all over your face. And your skin is kinda dewy-like, but not from just the humidity. It's different dewy. Why?"

"I—" I stumbled and tried pulling at my clothes subconsciously while I thought up a good enough lie. Usually they came to me easily, but not this time.

"Then, of course, there's the smell."

"The smell?" I shook my head.

"You smell like him. Or like he would if he hadn't showered in a day or two." I couldn't tell, but I think her eyes began to well up.

"How would you know what the hell Will Cianciola *smells* like, Teal?" I felt my face muscles get in their fighting stance, and shot down the new suspicions that were suddenly showing up in my mind.

"It doesn't matter." She loosened her jaw and took a breath like she was trying to regather herself. "I just want to find Huck and then go start my life… away from South Carolina. And away from you. It's time for me to go find another ocean."

"What is this craziness you're talkin', Teal? What do you mean you want to go find *another ocean*?" I mocked her drama. "Huck is missin'. I need you more than ever right now. You just gonna up and leave me?"

"I know you do, Mama. You always do. And of course, I'll help until we find Huck. I'll try my hardest to clean up some more of your messes."

"My messes!?" I felt my ears go hot.

"Yeah, Mom. Much like all of the other bad shit that goes on in our lives, this is all your fault," she stated coldly, arms folded.

"My fault!? You're the one who saw the Cianciola girl with some stranger and said nothin' to nobody!"

"Yeah, and that was stupid, but look at my raisin'."

I let the one insult slide. "Things like this are no one's fault, Teal. I wouldn't have hurt a hair on that kid's head, and neither would you."

"All you've ever done is hurt us, Mama." She said in a lower, colder tone.

"Now you take that back! Right damn now!"

"If you didn't make the most awful decisions about everythin'!" Her voice finally rose up to its tiptoes. "If you weren't always gettin' mixed up with these disgustin' men, like Hank Feller…if you weren't such an old desperate slut—"

I smacked her in the mouth. Hard. It didn't matter that maybe she was right. It mattered that I was her mother. It mattered that I was hurting, too, and in that weak moment, I acted. I hit my child.

"Nice," she said flatly as her face got red and hot in the shape of my hand. "Is that the cherry on top? You go screw Will, then come back over here to hit me in the face?"

"What do you care what I did with him so much? It ain't because you're worried he had somethin' to do with all this, is it?" I asked before she turned her back to me. "Did he do somethin' with you? While I was outta town? Somethin' happened, didn't it?" I inched toward her, my nostrils flared out ready to unleash the dragon's fire that I was now certain was inside of me.

She kind of scoff-smiled at me, and started to say something when someone started pecking on the door.

"Yoohoo, it's Karen. Are you in there, Miss Tracy?" The voice was high-pitched and perky. I immediately rolled my eyes.

"Who's Karen?" Teal asked, hands on her hips. "You bangin' her too?"

I shot her a warning look. "It's us, but for the Myrtle Beach area. She works for Limeberry, a property manager. So you better shut up and be nice."

"Just tell her we're fine and send her away. I don't want to see anybody right now." Teal leaned her head up against the wall, then banged it one good time for effect.

"Trust me, there is no sendin' Karen away. I'll be quick." I said before I jerked the door open after the repeated knocks set to the rhythm of "Pop Goes the Weasel."

"Hey, sweetie." The bubbly woman slightly shorter and rounder than me threw her arms around my neck. "Mr. Limeberry sent me out here to check on you and make sure you're getting settled in all right. I know you were down at the station most of the day yesterday. That couldn't have been fun, sweetie. Tell me, how are you feeling now? Is it just terrible?"

I felt like saying *hungover,* but instead I answered, "I'm doin' the best I can be. It's a whirlwind, really. I was just gonna shower up and head out to look with the search parties."

"Oh, honey. Is there anything at all that I can do to make you more comfortable?"

"I don't think that's even possible. Just keep your eyes open. Help look. It's what I've been sayin' to everybody." I gave her the closed mouth smile-nod, the one that let most people know to get moving. But, she didn't take the cue.

"Oh you've got it, sweetheart. Aww." she threw herself awkwardly around me once more, this time over my arms that were hanging by my side. It made me feel like a puppy being loved too hard by some eager kid in a pet store. "And your daughter is here, too, now, I understand? How's she doing, dear?"

"She's like me, as good as she can be. She's just sittin' over at the bar there." I turned my head to peer inside while she continued squeezing me. "Teal, come here and say hey, please." I heard her sigh deeply but get up anyway.

"Oh, that's all right. I'd hate—" Karen began shuffling backwards.

"Hi there—" Teal said, walking around from the other side of the door before she froze dead in her tracks.

"Teal?" I nudged her, finally free of Karen. "You all right? You look like you're fixin' to pass out or somethin', honey." I put a hand underneath her elbow in case.

"Oh, dear," Karen said, her big wide eyes growing even larger. "I better get going then. I didn't want to upset anybody."

Teal eased the door shut in her face, holding up her finger as if to say, *Give me a minute.*

"Just wait one second, Karen." I managed.

"Mama…" Teal said slowly.

"Teal, what are you doin'?" I reached to reopen the door, but she grabbed my wrist to stop me.

I could see her temples pulsing through her skin, and her chest was moving up and down at a rate I'd never seen anyone's move before. "Mama…" she whispered with eyes that had just seen a ghost.

"What, honey? For the love of God, what?" I took her by the shoulders and searched her terrified eyes.

"That's her," she whispered.

"Who? Who is it?" I could feel my own heart racing to catch up with hers, though I didn't yet know why.

"That's the woman I saw on the beach," she panted. "That's the woman I saw draggin' Chloe Cianciola off Folly by the arm, the woman I described to the sketch artist yesterday. She's standin' right there on our front porch."

CHAPTER 19

I froze for a second. Then I whispered to my daughter in the most serious voice I had, "Are you absolutely sure that's the woman you saw?"

Teal nodded slowly, her chest contracting up a storm, but her lips pressed together with crazy glue. The color had left her cheeks completely, and she only looked alive because she was nearly hyperventilating.

"Okay." I walked her to the bedroom just beyond the kitchen and sat her on the bed, my hands still on her shoulders. "Okay, here's what we're gonna do. I'm gonna go back out on the porch and chat her up as pretty and pleasant as you please. You are gonna call the police, and stay in this room until they get here. All right?" I was surprised at my calm demeanor. It was almost always Teal who did better in these situations, but seeing this woman's face was her tipping point, and I knew it. It was time to step up and pay my dues. It was time for me to do my best to be a mother, for her sake and Huck's.

"Yeah, yeah. That's good." Teal picked up the phone and dialed wildly.

I could hear the operator answer, "9-1-1. What is your emergency?" Then I made my way back into the living room, where I found Karen standing, still smiling from ear to ear, her bright shirt matching her cheeks. She looked like the president of the PTA, not a kidnapper.

Even so, I nearly jumped out of my skin when I saw her, "Oh, gosh, Karen...you startled me. I thought I'd left you out on the porch. Um, Teal is just not feelin', uh, very well. I think this is all just too much for her. But, why don't I make some tea, and the two of us can chit chat for a little while." I tried sounding as natural as I could as I took a couple peppy and unnatural steps toward the cupboards.

"Tell her to put the phone down, Tracy." Her tone lacked all of the bubbles it normally had.

"What?" I smiled awkwardly shaking my head, still reaching for the tea.

"Teal, it's Karen. Put the phone down, dear." She shouted through the house. "I have a gun, and I will use it on your mother here. And just think of what could become of little Huck." Her demeanor was eerie, insincerely cheerful, but also chilling to the bone.

"Okay, Karen, just calm down." I trembled with my hands stretched out toward the shiny baby Glock she now held in her hand.

Teal opened the bedroom door and tiptoed out, her hands also up, palms out, by her shoulders.

"I recognized you the second you came around that door facing. I just couldn't place from where at first. But I guess you didn't have the same problem, did you, honey?" she asked my frightened daughter. "You remembered quick, didn't you, love?"

Teal eased to my side, her eyes on Karen the whole time. Neither of us said a word.

"What are the odds?" Karen shook her head. "What were you doing down there so late in the evening anyway? I thought I'd be safe out there after the sun had gone down. Only mischievous little girls troll the beaches at night like that. Chloe had that spirit. She'd run off from her Daddy in the pitch black dark, not a lick of sense about her. It was in her nature; didn't even need to bait her. She'd have grown up to have been a mischievous little girl too. Just like you, Teal." Karen reached into her purse and pulled out her cell phone. "Always sticking your nose where it doesn't belong."

"Maybe we—" I tried to speak.

"Shut up!" Karen shouted, slamming the phone down onto the counter. "Get into the hall closet.

Both of you. Right now."

"Just go, Teal." I whispered, inching her toward the hallway. Then even quieter, "We'll think of somethin'."

Reluctantly, we got inside the closet and faced Karen, knowing more instructions would be on the way soon enough. I was actually relieved when she said, "Tie Teal's hands with that belt hanging there. Hurry." It was better than getting shot point blank right in the face.

After I bound my daughter, it was my turn. Karen held the gun on me with one hand and made a loop using her free hand and her teeth with a second belt. Then she tightened it over my own wrists that she had demanded I hold behind my back. Once she secured me to her liking, she sat the gun down and tied both of our feet up, one a robe tassel and the other with a tie she found lying on the floor beside us. I had the strangest thought that whoever had left the random stuff behind in the vacation rental could never have imagined what they'd later be used for. They'd probably come down to the ocean from some colder, landlocked place like Iowa, and had had the time of their lives in that little townhouse. Now it had become my own personal hell, and Teal's too. It was worse than a prison cell, and I was scared it might even become the little corner of the world where we'd draw our last breaths…a new coffin that was painted stark white and had a couple wire coat hangers swinging overhead. And that scared me in a way that there aren't words made to describe, in a way that could only be felt, and never communicated to someone else.

"I don't want to hear a peep out of either of you." Karen picked up the gun then slammed the door behind her, leaving us in total blackness. Then I heard her set something down in exchange for something else. The gun for the phone, maybe? I couldn't be sure.

"Teal, I'm scared. I'm so scared." I whispered to my daughter, losing some of that backbone I thought I'd built up. "I—I know you're mad at me right now, but I wish you could reach out and grab my hand…like you did when you were little if I was cryin' over some asshole. I—"

"I know, I know, Mama. But be strong," she said. "Just be quiet now. We'll get through it. I got the call out. I couldn't speak, but they should be able to trace it soon. I tried to let them hear me breathe, so they'd know somebody was there. Just hold on. We'll get out of this. Believe that they are comin', okay? Believe it hard with me."

"Why are you always the strong one?" I whispered as softly as I could, trying my best not to get choked up.

And she said nothing. My Teal just sat there, solid as a rock like always. She regained her bravery almost as fast as I'd lost mine again.

On the other side of the door I heard Karen speaking to someone in a low voice. "The daughter saw me that night we acted on Chloe. I don't know what to do. She recognized me. I've got 'em tied up in the closet now. Are you still just next door? I need you to get over here, right now."

"Oh, dear God." I cupped my hand over my mouth. "Will." I mumbled into it, tears threatening me with their burning stings. It was just like the first few brushes from a jellyfish tentacle before it latched on all the way, paralyzing you right where you stood.

Teal said nothing, but I heard her let out the tiniest, most pitiful whimper. It wasn't one with as much shock as hurt…a deeply personal, stabbed-in-the-heart, hurt.

"All right, hurry!" Karen demanded, then, "To hell if they see your face! For all I know the cops could be here any second. Teal was in the back room when I got in. I don't know if she made the call or not. But we've got to do something about them, and we've got to do it right now. The little act is over." I heard her slam the phone down, and cock the gun hard and fast—the most haunting sound in all the world.

PART 3

WILL

CHAPTER 20

"Don't be a coward," I said out loud to myself, pulling my white t-shirt over my head in front of the mirror. "Just walk over there and deal with this, Will. Face the music."

I filled my cheeks up with air and slowly blew it out again, closing my eyes and regaining my composure. Then I reached and grabbed for the cheap brassy doorknob. It was time; time to walk over there and clean up the mess I'd made, so I could focus on what needed to be done. I had one task ahead of me that I'd now muddied up with all kinds of dirt. I'd made the water so murky that I couldn't even see through it anymore. It had become a swamp stocked full of creatures ready to eat me alive, and I'd done it to myself. So it was up to me to clear it. I could at least be man enough to fix it, finish it, and get out of this horrible mess I had made for so many people.

It had all started out so simple. I'd just needed a change. I was sick of Watertown. I was sick of smelling Jessica's perfume lingering in the cobwebbed corners of the upstairs closet, embedded into the handful of blouses she'd left behind. I was sick of working as a contractor in New England in the winter with the thigh-high snow. I was sick of the cold brick house with no parking that Jess had picked out because it was just 'so charming.' Truth was that it was 300 years old, overpriced, and needed new plumbing like hell needed rain. And after she left, it was my prison. I hated that house and everything it represented. I hated the big bay windows that only opened to concrete, and that sick pale yellow color that looked like bile. She loved it; said it reminded her of a songbird. But the only songs that came out of that house were sad requiems made up of what our lives had become. I wished that it would just fall apart around me at times, but it was built too strong for that. I knew in my bones that it would stand forever, mysterious and full of dark history, like Stonehenge or some other ruins too full of some sinister power to ever fall.

My days were all the same back in Watertown. My life had started to feel like a sick sequel to "Groundhog Day" set in Middlesex County, Massachusetts. I'd get up, and notice it was cold again, make Chloe an egg and three for myself. Then I'd take Chloe to her shitty public school and warn her not to fall on the rusty slide. After that I'd go off to build various things for richer men than myself...the kind that tried to give me little undermining nicknames like they'd called their childhood dog. After they'd referred to me as "Sport" or "Champ" and worked their degrees from Harvard into our brief conversations about the additions to their homes, they'd trot off into the city with their Mont Blanc suitcases in hand and Armani suits draped onto their white, doughy bodies. I hated all of them. I didn't fit with any of them. But, then again, I didn't fit anywhere at that point.

I couldn't go back to my old friends from Southie either. I didn't want to end up in a basement boxing for money again while guys bet on me like a prized cock in an abandoned warehouse. Worse than that, I didn't want to get my ass kicked for leaving by my old acquaintances? Friends wasn't the right word. They'd had big dreams for me after I'd retired from the prestigious underground fighting rings...like joining their businesses selling crack or ripped off pistols, the ones that weren't behind bars by then, anyway.

I think that my past was part of why I'd married Jess to begin with. She was from a good family, in a better part of town where they had HOAs and trees on the sidewalks. She was from one of those families that had traced their heritage back to England and had great grandfathers with Sir printed in front of their names. She made me want to be better, stay away from the riff raff, and stop trying to be an 80s-era Wahlberg. But then, sometimes I thought that fighting in Southie might have turned out to have been better for me than she was. I'd have ended up being either a hero or a dead man, and neither of those things would have hurt as bad as being abandoned, stuck, and then just alone. Jess had just teased me with her normal family, dinners at six and hopes for the future. None of it was enough to keep her mood up. I'd been that thing once without realizing it; the Southie bad boy that made her feel alive. And I couldn't be it again. Instead I tried to be the husband that would stand by her, and the father a little girl would be proud to have.

It wasn't enough. Nothing was enough to make her want to get the help she really needed and stay with us. It had just been enough to start the process, get her to try a little, and then leave me spinning somewhere in the middle of it all, picking up all the pieces without any help.

I was left there in the middle. I wasn't rich or poor. I wasn't in the worst part of town or the best. I wasn't loved or hated. I wasn't anything but Chloe's pitiful dad whose wife had run out on him. I was that single dad who held it together on the outside while everyone gave out their pitied looks as some sort of sick gift handed out on the street corners. They all thought that somehow I'd feel cared for if they offered me their bizarre smile-frowns from the side of the road as I passed by, as though their sorrow communicated just the right way would help me somehow. It was an odd offering, though, like the flower I was given as a boy from a Hare Krishna at the airport. I felt like accepting the pity would only make me more vulnerable, and more pathetic.

So I got drunk one night after a day of a particularly high number of sad faces directed at me, and started googling "America's best cities on the ocean." I was just dreaming of sunnier, warmer places like everyone else did in New England by late February. After the duds that were Miami and Seattle, I stumbled across Charleston, South Carolina, and got drawn in. It wasn't big and fast-paced like Miami, or gloomy and melancholy like Seattle. Charleston was like what would have happened if Boston had lived…if there'd been warm days instead of cold, if there'd been double-decker side verandas instead of porchless salt boxes, or if there'd been palm trees and Spanish moss instead of red oaks that were bare for most of the year. Charleston was what would have happened if Boston got high on magic mushrooms and started seeing pastel colors on the trip. And at the time it seemed to be exactly what I needed. It would fix everything.

The next thing I knew, I was on Indeed looking for job postings. I came across an ad for Limeberry Properties, headquartered in nearby Folly Beach. They needed a new project manager for communities in development all up and down the warm South Carolina coast. The pay was good and would get me a lot more down south than it ever would have up north. I'd be working from Hilton Head Island all the way up to Myrtle Beach. The weather was mild year-round, it never snowed, and three quarters of the days in a year were bright and sunny. Best of all, there'd be no reminders of Jess, or dank basements, or schools covered in ivy. The worst I'd come across would be a few insincere old ladies trying to bless my heart while they told me about their grandson at Clemson. Anyone could deal with that. It was perfect.

I was three sheets to the wind when I sent my application in. The next morning when I woke up, hung over as all hell, I laughed at the idea, then never gave it a second thought. Honestly, I wasn't sure if I'd attached my resume to that email or a copy of my fantasy football draft notes. But it didn't matter. It was just some dumb, drunken whim. So I got up, chugged a bottle of water, and started my "Groundhog Day" routine as usual.

I'd forgotten about the whole thing two weeks later by the time I got the phone call while shoveling out the driveway one evening. Two phone interviews and a Skype later, I was packing my bags. Chloe and I stuck a *for sale* sign through the snow into the patchy front yard of Jessica's house, and moved on to warmer beaches. I decided that we'd drift up and down the coast, in no hurry to settle anywhere in particular over the summer. But when we got there, I never found that freedom I'd been looking for. I realized that it wasn't the brick house that had been my prison. It had been my life, and my sentence was nowhere near over. And now, maybe I was set to serve life.

CHAPTER 21

I finally got ahold of my balls and pecked on the door of the unit two doors down from mine. When I thought of facing both Teal and Tracy on the other side, I could feel my pores opening up to let the sweat push through. I was sure I'd be shiny from head to toe, like I'd gone and covered myself in Vaseline by the time I saw them. I only hoped not. I hated showing my nerves. One of my stepdads used to tell me it was a sign of weakness. He'd rub my shoulders from the corner of the ring when he started me fighting for cash at thirteen. He'd say, "Never let 'em see you sweat, and you'll be fine, kid." I don't know why I could do it so much better then than now. Because now I had soaked through my shirt. I could even see the shine on my knuckles when I made a fist to knock on the door.

"Finally." The door swung open creating a

breeze.

"Oh, Karen..." I felt the confusion settle between my eyes. "Did you come by to check on—" My voice trailed when I saw it. "Why in God's name do you have...a gun? Are you all right? Where are Teal and Tracy?" My eyes bounced off every wall in two seconds.

"What are you doing here?" She held up the pistol less than confidently and pointed it directly at me.

My hands eased up into the air. "I—I came to talk to Teal and Tracy. I just needed to clear the air about some stuff that happened between me and them. What in God's name? Where are they, Karen?" I spoke carefully.

"They're in the closet where you're going to go too." She paused. "Move it. The hall closet. Now."

"Okay, okay." I held my hands up again. "I'm going. I haven't done anything wrong, Karen. If something has happened, we should call the police."

"Shut up," she snapped. "Take your belt off and give it to me. Right now. No funny business. I swear to God I'll shoot you right here." I complied, my mind racing through a hundred different scenarios.

She had me put my wrists together and hold them behind my back. She held the gun with one hand while she struggled to tighten the belt around my wrists with the other, but she managed. She then opened the closet where I saw two pairs of crystal blue eyes staring at me, both sets as wide as the full moon. They said nothing with their mouths, but the eyes spoke for them. They were as scared and confused as I was and had no idea what to do.

"If any of you even breathe loudly enough for me to hear it, I'll just start firing at this door until I'm empty. Not a sound! Understand me?" We all nodded wildly as Karen slammed it shut with a force her rather small stature didn't look like it was capable of bringing. I then heard her wedge a chair up underneath the doorknob before I heard another voice slice into the air, calling out her name.

"Karen? Where are you?" The voice echoed through the house, barely audible by the time it made it to me.

"God. I didn't think you'd ever get here." She sounded out of breath. "I'm really freaking out here, man. There's three of 'em now. What are we gonna do?"

"What do you mean three? Who else?" The muffled but familiar voice demanded.

"Will Cianciola peddled ass over here while I was waiting on you, and I opened the door. They're all in the closet now. I tied 'em up and told 'em I'd shoot if they made a peep."

"All right. First of all, we've gotta get 'em out of here. You go pull the van around back. Give me the gun. We'll load 'em up and take 'em to the storage unit where we're holding the boy. We can take care of business there. It'll be way too messy if we try to do anything here. Too many nosy neighbors poking around. It'd be a huge and stupid risk that could ruin everything."

When the voice said this Teal and Tracy began to scream through tears, and jerk at their binds. I couldn't tell which one was more frantic.

"Stop. Just stop," I whispered. "I heard it too. If they were talking about Huck, you have even the more reason not to panic. You don't want to end up dead. Be smart."

"I'm—I'm tryin'." Teal whispered through sobs.

"Now who's voice is that? It's so familiar to me. I wish I could hear him better." I stretched my neck out in the dark.

"I—I can barely make it out. I just heard him say something about the boy and a storage unit. Do you think he really *is* talkin' about Huck? I mean, it has to be Huck, right?" Teal croaked.

"I can't hear him at all now...I—I'm not sure," Tracy said. "But if he *is* tryin' to take us to where Huck is, then Will is right; we need to try to make it there alive. So be quiet!" I could tell Tracy's sudden decision to be the voice of reason didn't set well with Teal. I couldn't see her face, but it was like I could feel the warmth from her cheeks that I knew were on fire.

I pressed my ear up to my side of the closet where I thought I heard Karen opening the back porch door. Then there was silence. I pressed my ear harder against the cold plywood. And just when nearly all of my weight was against it, it swung open, causing me to fall hardly onto my shoulder. I heard Tracy and Teal both gasp and cry out in perfect unison as I struggled up off of my bound arms.

The voice shouted out, "Shut up, and listen!" And this time it was as clear as a bell. I knew exactly who Karen's partner was before I even looked up.

CHAPTER 22

"Limeberry," I whispered, then struggled to my feet with my hands still belted behind my back.

"Oh, my god. We trusted you." Tracy wept by her daughter. "You're the one…you and that Karen, if that's even her real name. It was you!" She was shouting by the end of the sentence.

"I didn't want it to go this way, Will. But I'm a man who believes in good business, and you, my friend… you're now in the middle of my business." He pointed the gun into my face, his fat arm draping over his ballooned gut. "You were my best contractor too. Such a damn shame. I had a feeling I'd need to follow you up here and keep an eye out…you're so vol-a-tile." He drew the word out in born and bred South Carolina style.

"Where's my daughter, you son-of-a—" I

couldn't even get it all out. I didn't know if the lump in my throat got too large or if it had something to do with the fact that his hand was now around my throat, and the cold metal barrel of the gun was resting not so gently against my pulsing temple.

"Just calm down, Cianciola. There aren't a lot of ways this can work out for you now, buddy. And we both know it. But, see, I still have my queen in this little chess game we've entered into, and you're down to all pawns, Bud. I've got your girl." He grinned like a hyena, a toothpick still resting in a gap between his yellowing bottom teeth.

I clenched my jaw tightly, trying hard not to let out the whimpers I could hear escaping from Teal and Tracy. I could never give him that satisfaction. So I dug my feet in and focused my eyes, just like I had all of those years with leather gloves hurling toward my face.

"How does this end with us alive?" I growled.

"It doesn't," Limeberry said in the good-Baptist version of his Southern drawl, yet somehow still cold and flat. "That would be bad for business. You'll make your promises not to go to the police and plead for your life, but ultimately, if you all stay alive, I'll end up getting caught. And we can't have that, can we?"

I couldn't see the look on Teal or Tracy's face, and I was glad for it. I didn't want to know what a woman's face looked like when she was told emphatically that her life was going to end. However, I *could* hear the pitiful wincing, which was almost just as bad.

Limeberry never flinched. He just continued with his eerily calm speech. "But this can end with you getting to see your kids again, and them getting a chance at a life. I could kill you all now." He motioned with the weapon. "Shoot you somewhere unpleasant on the body that will bleed out slowly...the spleen or something." He spoke like a deadpan comedian, and was pleased with it. "We could make the big scene, and everybody end up on the news. Of course, I'll have to go to a lot of effort to make it look like I stumbled onto the crime scene. That will involve a whole change of clothes, throwing away things, stashing the murder weapon, planting fingerprints. God, maybe even bleach, depending on how the blood splatter lands. Messy, messy. It will take all evening, and I'll miss the rest of the golf tournament I had going on the TV when I was interrupted with all this chaos. Then, of course, I will go auction your children, as planned, to the highest bidder who will do what they wish with them. I don't know or care where they'll end up. They may get sold again, or used for personal amusement of some type. Or if they have a rare blood type, maybe something interesting in medicine. It gets rather hairy. I prefer not to think about it. I'm simply the dealer. Once the car is driven off the lot, it's no longer my business if somebody wrecks it, you know?"

"You're soulless," I forced through my gnashed teeth staring into his thick transitional bifocals that only made his big round head more hideous to look at.

"Actually, I'm not. Here's why." He held his finger in the air and spoke in a way that was more for his enjoyment than for ours. "If you all make this a little easier on me, and calmly get into the van Karen is pulling around back, quiet as the little mice you are...I will not only let you say goodbye to your children, but I will let them go. They haven't seen my face. They don't know where they are, nor do they understand what is happening. I'll lose two sales, but that's okay because I have other irons in the fire. After you say goodbye, I will kill you quickly and painlessly, and of course, out of the sight of your children. It'll be lights out so fast you'll never know what happened. And your kids will go on to live another day. I'll just have them driven to a populated area in an unmarked car and let out somewhere. They'll find family members to take them in from some place, or if there is no family, the very best foster families are sure to want them. And they'll get paid to tell their strange tale to Oprah here in a few years, which should help pay for college. Everybody wins. I can be quite the giver when I want to be, you see. After all, this got messier than I'd hoped, and you all were valued employees of mine. I never wanted our professional relationships to suffer. Just think of my generosity as a little severance package of sorts." He smiled like a dirty politician.

I glanced over at Teal and Tracy, their watering eyes pleading with me to do something. My mind raced. Flashes of Chloe running away from me with that red sand bucket danced cruelly in front of my eyes, so alive, yet so far away...in another realm, not like a ghost, but like a life on a whole different plane, living and breathing. I thought of her. If I could give my life for hers, if Limeberry would only keep his end of the deal, I'd do it. I'd do it in a second.

"What's it gonna be, Cianciola? Teal, Tracy?" He eyed all three of us. "Have we reached an agreement, here? Time is ticking. I fear the boys in blue will be along soon."

The problem was, he wouldn't keep his promise. He'd kill us somewhere more convenient for him and continue with his so-called "business." If he did even still have our kids, they would end up on whatever underground market he was a part of, and the three of us would end up in the bellies of swamp gators. He didn't know that we'd heard him talking to Karen. He'd told her that we were being taken to the place where "the boy" was being held. The storage units. That meant it was within driving distance, hours at the very most. The police could find the kids with that information, and now we knew at least one child, hopefully Huck, was there for sure. I couldn't risk it. I had a chance right then to find my daughter. I knew what I had to do. I had to catch him off guard. I had to fight. I had to channel whatever ounce of South Boston I still had stirring around inside of me, and bring it back from the dead. I had to perform a resurrection of who I used to be, taking blows from grown men at thirteen years old. I had to fight again, in one more dark room, one more place, fuming with total desperation, and for the prize of my life.

"All right, we'll go with you." I bluffed. "We'll get in the van, and we'll go quietly. I want to see the kids set free before you do what you have to do with us though. Is that a deal?"

"You have my word." Limeberry said it so sincerely, believing *I* had believed him.

Tracy and Teal sat behind me, their faces pale and eyes unblinking. I shot them a look that did its best to communicate to them that I had a plan.

"I want you to leave the gun here as a showing of good faith." I said. "You won't need it. We don't want anything to happen to the kids. Plus, we're all tied up."

Limeberry laughed and looked at his shoes. "Not gonna happen, Cianciola. Sorry. You're a funny guy though, I'll hand ya that. You got me plumb tickled with that one, now."

"I just want to know you aren't gonna take us somewhere and kill us before letting the kids go. You can leave us tied up. The girls have their hands *and* feet tied. You can tie my feet too. We won't try to escape because we won't be able to bound up like we are. And if we were to try anything funny, we know you won't tell us where the children are being held."

"It's not gonna happen, Will. It's my way or no way, buddy boy. No room for negotiations. There's no way in hell I'm transporting you if I'm unarmed." He paused. "Now get on your fucking feet. I can see that my amenable attitude has led you to believe you can haggle with me. Either that, or you're stalling. I won't listen to any more of this horseshit, so get up! All of you, move! Back door, now." He shouted in case we were worried he'd gotten too agreeable.

"Tracy and Teal still have their feet tied," I pointed out, stalling still, Catholic prayers reciting themselves in the back of my mind.

"They can wiggle onto their feet and hop just fine. They better fucking figure it out, at least." He pointed the gun toward them then back to me, starting to look a little shaken, aware that seconds were passing, and that cops could be on their way.

We all scrambled to get up, Teal and Tracy working the hardest. Teal made it up first, using the wall to brace herself, and sobbing the whole time. I was next, making it to my knees, then feet, one at a time. Tracy struggled the worst. She remained on the ground, losing all her wits. Her crying was getting louder by the second, and I could tell she was about to snap like a twig in November. She was going to lose what little cool she had and get one or all of us shot right then and there.

"Hurry up, you skinny bitch! Use some muscle!" Limeberry screamed at her, pointing the gun at her face as it struggled from where it was pressed against the cold floor. Then he turned to Teal. "Wiggle over there and let her lean on your shoulder. If you don't get her crying ass off the ground, I'm gonna start spraying bullets."

Teal hopped toward her mother like a three-legged puppy in an alley, searching my face for help along the short but tedious trip. It was pitiful to watch when Limeberry started to chuckle at her, but his cruelty became my moment to act. He took his eye off of me for too many seconds in a row. He raised the gun and rested it on his chin casually while he laughed like a fat bully on a third grade playground. And I did it. I took my opportunity and lurched toward him with all of my strength. I took all of my pain from the night Chloe was taken and balled it up into a potent little pill and swallowed it, letting it open up inside of my body, and drive the momentum out of my skin. I tackled him with all the force of my bound being and headbutted him as hard as I could on the way down.

Teal and Tracy both screamed out as we fell to the floor. The adrenaline coursed through my body in a way it never had before. I saw the faces of every guy twice my age and size that I'd headbutted before him, laughing gap-toothed at the skinny bastard-born teenager from Southie whom they never thought stood a chance. Their taunts rang through my ears, and in that moment might as well have all been Limeberry. It was like they were just little particles of one ugly soul that joined forces and then became the ultimate beast I had to slay for my last rite of passage. And I would slay him then if it killed me. Every piece of my life formed the whole man I was to become, finally, in the very moment I needed the power to prevail. I was stronger than I'd ever been. Every punch I'd taken, every blow Southie had given me inside the ring or out stood up to cheer me on—getting my ass kicked my first twenty fights, growing up on food stamps, losing Jess, losing Chloe, becoming a suspect, that sick laugh of his.

After the initial headbutt, the fire inside of me

had been set. It now blazed out of control and fueled me so that I was able to loosen one of my hands from where they were restrained. When it broke free, I grabbed for the gun while Limeberry and I cut somersaults across the sandy floor. I could hear the girls screaming and could see them struggling with their own restraints out of the corner of my eye when I heard it…the loud piercing pop inches from my ear that cut all the way through me to the noise that only existed inside of my own head. Then the beasts at battle were silenced, and the energies in the air fled as fast as they had shown up. All I could see was blackness, and all I could hear was a ringing. And everything went still.

CHAPTER 23

I couldn't hear the sirens for the ringing in my ears. The noise in my head was so thick I would have sworn to the Pope that it was a real live thing, some animal, with a mass and a heartbeat. It was more than just a deafening and painful noise. It was worse than taking a bare-knuckle right hook straight to the ear. The noise was warm, reverbing off the walls in my skull and pulsing bigger and bigger by the minute. It was a noise that could also be felt. I think it triggered senses I'd never used before, that I didn't know humans had.

I remembered the feeling of being tackled by one of the police officers, getting slammed to my stomach while I watched Limeberry bleed out through his stupid purple golf shirt. The gun had fallen out of my hand by this time. But was it ever really in my hand? I wasn't sure. I just remember it being tangled up between the two of us when it went off. Maybe I'd pulled the trigger; maybe he had. I'd never know. But in those short moments I mulled it over as much as I ever would.

Then I saw it, the blood running out of the side of my neck where the pain was losing its initial numbness. My neck had felt oddly muted at first, but now I could feel it all screaming out of me, another sense coming back to life with more power than it had had before. That heat was leaving, and all I was starting to feel was cold.

The bullet had ricocheted some way between Limeberry and me, as close as our bodies had been. That had to have been what happened. I'd only heard one pop. That, I was sure of. I didn't know who was hit first, but we were both losing blood rapidly. I could see his gushing out maybe even more than I could feel my own. The confused cops scrambled to help us both, but I, the known suspect, was being handled with the most caution…and the roughest. When my hearing finally returned a bit, I noticed my voice had left. I wanted to scream out everything I knew to the officers about "the boy" being held at some storehouse, about Limeberry's disgusting business, about now knowing who stole my Chloe…but my throat would not move. They knew nothing of what had just happened. They just knew people were tied up, the figurehead mayor of the coast was bleeding out, and I was in the middle of all of it.

The officers scattered, some toward me and some toward Limeberry.

I heard one officer shout, "Who did this to you? Was it Cianciola? Can you hear us, Mr. Limeberry?"

Teal and Tracy shouted back at him incoherently before more officers rushed to untie them. The one holding me down like I was a common crook finally stopped looking wildly around the room and noticed the blood rushing out of my neck.

His eyes widened to silver dollars and he screamed out "Get me a couple busses out here now! Cianciola's been hit too."

It wasn't happening in slow motion like it does on all the crime TV shows. It was all incredibly fast—the sharp noises, the rushing blood, the drawn guns in every corner. It was a tornado moving at record-breaking speed through the tiny townhouse, sucking every one of us up into the violent vortex.

At some point, probably after two seconds, I felt the cop move the pressure from my arms to the actual wound. He had both hands pressed down hard on the hole in my neck. The pressure seared into me like a hot fire stoker, but I knew that maybe that force would be the thing to save my life. Also in that moment, I was strangely aware that I wanted to live. I just wanted to live, and that was the biggest shock of the whole thing. I could feel my mind and body fighting for it with everything.

"Oh God. Save him, please! Don't let him die!" I heard Teal scream out. "He didn't do this! Please, please!"

"Stay calm, ma'am. We're doing what we can," a voice said, not so calm, itself.

"God, please! I love him!" she sob-screamed.

"You what?" Tracy cried, confused and pitiful.

"Just breathe, and let us work." Another more paced voice spoke from somewhere. "We're doing everything we—"

And silence.

CHAPTER 24

When I opened my eyes, all I could see was the color blue. It was everywhere, splashed liberally throughout all of space. Then I blinked. Once, twice, and a third time for good measure. Other things started coming into focus. There was a television screen in the corner, a lady with bobbed blonde hair and the whitest teeth I'd ever seen mouthing something from behind a news desk. Then the clear tubes showed up. The clear tubes were everywhere. On the fourth blink, the first naturally occurring one, I saw the blue again, but smaller this time. I'd found the source of it perched at the end of my bed, sitting on the stark white blanket. Teal's eyes were staring down at me, smiling somehow, even though her mouth wasn't. Then came her voice.

"Will!? Will, can you hear me?" She frantically

pushed a button in her hand.

"Teal?" I asked groggily.

"Will, it's me. I'm right here. You're all right." Her thick drawl filled the room.

Then a voice answered through a speaker on the railing, "Yes. This is Julie."

"He's awake. He said my name this time. I think he's really back," Teal replied hurriedly.

I lifted my hand gently and felt the bandage on my neck from where the pain radiated. Almost immediately when I touched it, the memories came marching in like stern soldiers doing that eerie goose step in a single file line. I saw the fastest montage of a cold Boston day, my mother's burnt meatloaf, Jessica laughing with her head thrown back, Chloe smiling with a missing tooth, Teal holding herself...and then Mr. Limeberry, that disgusting chuckle of his, the gun going off, and, of course, the darkness.

"Oh, my god. Where is...what happened—" I tried to sit up. "I was shot...I know I was shot..."

"Easy there, cowboy." A calm voice, Julie's, I'm assuming, said as she gently pushed me back toward the pillow. It didn't take much either. Almost all of my strength was gone. The petite nurse might as well have thrown a feather at me, but it was enough. "Just relax while we check out all of your vitals, okay?"

"How—how long have I been out?" I asked.

"What day is it?"

The nurse chuckled. "You've only been here a day, and you've only been out about two hours this time. You've already opened your eyes for us a few times and mumbled a little bit here and there…just nothing that's made any sense yet. You've had visitors and everything. See all the flowers and balloons?" She looked around as if she, too, were seeing them all for the first time.

"What visitors? Who would come see *me*?"

"Well, Teal here, hasn't left your side. Her mama has been through, too, and the chaplains. We made an exception for the McHones to see you since there was no next of kin. We thought you could use some sort of comforting presence in the room."

"Am I gonna die?" I mumbled, my eyes still blurry.

"Oh, heavens, no." The nurse responded. "You did lose some blood, but I'll let the doctor explain all that to you. You're just still feeling the effects of the anesthesia. It's why you're so confused. Last time I was in here you weren't able to tell me your name, the year, and your location. Do you think you can tell me that this time?"

"Uh…William Cianciola. 2020. And I guess I'm at the hospital in Surfside Beach."

"They sent you up here to Myrtle, but you were out like a light then, so close enough! Good job." She flashed a light in my eyes and had me follow her finger back and forth before she noted her findings in a beige chart.

Then it hit me like a thunderbolt, sobering me up. "Oh, my god. Chloe! Did they find Chloe?" I tried again to sit up. "There's a storage building. Limeberry said something about it. Before the scuffle. Was she there?"

The nurse gently pushed my shoulder back to my pillow again. "Hey now, we'll answer all of your questions, but you don't need to get all worked up again. You just had your neck sewn back together, Evel Knievel. You need to rest so that you heal up nicely for us, okay?"

"Look lady, what I need is my daughter. Tell me what happened. There's no chance of me relaxing until you do!" I raised my voice as much as it would let me, which wasn't what I was aiming for. I was confused and livid. I just wanted answers. I didn't want to be *handled* by anyone.

"Um—excuse me, but is it okay if I talk to my friend alone for a second?" Teal's twangy southern voice popped up in that unique way it did, like a fish springing up out of murky lake. "I think I can handle this if I just walk him through what happened…slowly, of course."

The nurse looked at me and then at Teal. "I don't know. The police told us that they wanted to talk to him before anyone else once he was able to do so. They told me to let them know as soon as he was fully coherent. Honestly, you shouldn't have been in here to begin with, but I knew he didn't have anyone. I don't want to get into any trouble."

"I'm just asking for a couple of minutes to be his friend. He's been through so much; more than any human should ever have to endure. I won't upset him, I promise," Teal all but pled.

The nurse sighed, "I won't make you leave the room. But I am not going to lie to the police. I'm letting them know that he seems to be ready to talk. You have until they arrive, and then it's out of my hands. I'll just go look in on my next patient for a couple minutes." She raised her eyebrows then dropped them again before leaving the room.

Teal reached out and smoothed my hair before she began, trying to figure out how to begin, her unlined face as furrowed as it could be. I felt like I was reading her mind somehow, and I knew she needed a nudge.

"Just start talking…" I said gently, shooting her a look to let her know it was okay.

"Will, first of all, I am *so* glad that you're okay." She grabbed my hand. "I know that you might still be mad at me about not going to the police sooner about everythin', and I'm so sorry about the way I handled that. I hope you can forgive me someday. I was scared. I thought I might have been wrong about it, and...you know, there's no excuse. It was just wrong not to come forward, but when I thought you might be dead, it broke me. I just had to come be with you, make sure you're all right."

I didn't have a response to that yet. Whatever went on between Teal and me was real, and it was big, but it had to sit in the backseat until I knew what had happened.

"There was so much blood...you passed out because there was so much." She went on. "I thought you were gone. You were just so pale and still by the time the paramedics got there. But the doctors got you into surgery fast. The bullet barely missed your jugular, and they say you're gonna be okay now. It'll take a lot of rest to fully heal, but they don't think you're gonna have any lastin' issues from this. You got a lot of blood from strangers runnin' through you now, though."

"I don't care about that, Teal. That isn't what I want to know, and you know it. Did they *find* Chloe? Or Huck?" I could feel myself panting like a dog. "Did they get to that storage unit?"

She paused for a moment and just stared at me. I knew the news wasn't good, and I blocked all the things that it could be, just waiting for her to speak. Then I would deal with it. Whatever they'd found or not found. Life, death, or nothing at all.

"Just say it," I squeezed my eyes shut.

She had such a simple chain of words to answer my question with, yet I could see she had to use all her strength to work her tongue. Finally, the courage came. "No, Will. They didn't find anythin'."

CHAPTER 25

I swallowed hard and looked up at the drop tile ceiling from my hospital bed, because I wasn't able to look directly at Teal. It pained my neck when I did it, like taking a fist straight to the throat. I didn't want to see the sorrow that I knew would be written all over her face.

"Will, it doesn't mean they won't find them," Teal said. "They just haven't yet." "So, no Huck, either?" I squeezed my eyes shut again.

"Not yet." She barely spoke loud enough for me to hear her. "No Huck, either."

"Tell me what happened. Everything. And don't leave anything out like you apparently like to do sometimes. I can take it...whatever it is." I didn't need anybody tiptoeing around me at this point. I didn't trust Teal not to hold something back if she thought it would protect me or maybe even herself.

"Okay." Teal looked away just as I finally decided to make eye contact. "I guess that's fair."

"You're damn right, it's fair. I might not be in this hospital bed right now if you'd told someone what you saw that night. My daughter might not *still* be a missing person."

"I know that. And I'm sorry, Will. I beat myself up about it every second of the day. I was scared—scared of being wrong, of being involved, of looking stupid. I was scared of all of the reasons there were to be scared. I'm not saying that any of it is a good excuse, which is why I didn't try to explain before, but it's what happened. It's the truth. I am sorry. Once I came to my senses, I tried to make it as right as I could."

"It's not good enough." I stiffened up my jaw.

"Yeah. I know that." She paused, and I think almost quizzed me about what happened between me and her mother, but she knew it wasn't the time. So instead she asked, "So do you want to know what happened or not?"

I shook my head yes, eyes once again glued to the drop tile ceiling.

"After you passed out, everythin' was just a whirlwind. The cops didn't know who had shot who. They were runnin' around tryin' to save lives and get the facts all at once. You and Limeberry were both out cold, and Mama and I were still partly tied up. It was chaos. They didn't even realize Karen was out back until it was too late."

"Did she get away?" I asked, still stiff in the jaw.

"They're lookin' for her. There's a huge manhunt in progress right now, but yes. She got away."

"And Limeberry?"

"Limeberry is dead." She paused. "So I imagine that the police will have some questions for you about that."

"Excellent." I didn't flinch, but began to picture another interrogation where some guy with coffee breath bounces between acting like my best friend and screaming into my face.

"But Mama and I told them everythin'. We told them that Mr. Limeberry was behind everythin', and that you were a victim too. We explained that Limeberry said he was gonna kill us and that you were wrestlin' him when the gun went off. I know they're gonna need your statement, but I really don't think they suspect you anymore. They seemed to believe us. They've turned every Limeberry office and property on its head lookin' for any kind of a clue. I don't know much. They've told us very little about that part. I only know that it appears as though Limeberry was some sort of middleman in a larger organization. They won't tell me who or what. I overheard somethin' about it being connected to one of the cartels, but I think that's only a theory. They're still diggin.'"

I nodded then asked, "What about the supposed storage unit he was talking about? Are the police looking for something in his name or in Limeberry Properties' name? Are they following up with that?"

"There were a couple of units in Limeberry's name, but they didn't find anythin' at either of them. It was all legit. Furniture and stuff like that." Her voice became a whisper. "I was really disappointed about that too. I believed in every part of my body that they'd be there. But maybe there's another unit out there, in another name or somethin'. I just don't know. He was referring to an actual place when he said it, I know he was."

"They're never going to find those kids, are they?" I finally got choked up. "They could be anywhere in the world by now."

"I know." Teal met me with her own tears. "But they are still lookin' at abandoned storage areas, units in Karen's name, empty units, warehouses. Everywhere they can think to look, they're lookin'."

"It's not enough. The world is too big and full of cracks for people to slip into," he croaked.

"We can't give up hope yet; it's all we have. I *heard* Limeberry say he wanted to take us to where they were holdin' the boy. He didn't know that we could hear him talkin'. He didn't make that up; it wouldn't make any sense for him to. It makes me believe that they are out there somewhere. They're a needle in a haystack, but one right underneath our noses. It's just like when I'm combin' the beach for a distinct shell or a specific fossil. I might need a shark's tooth exactly a quarter of an inch long to match another one just perfectly for a set of earrings. Or I need a flawlessly preserved Great White vertebrae, strong enough to drill through. I know they're there. They have to be. If I just keep searchin' at low tide when everything is revealed, I know I'll eventually have what I need. It's all there waitin' for me to find it and make somethin' beautiful out of it. Just like Huck and Chloe. They're waitin' on us too."

"I want to believe that. I do, Teal." I tried to conjure up all the faith I could, but I was always more logical than I was hopeful. "It's just….she's been gone even longer than Huck has. And I know neither of them have good odds. I don't want to spend my life wishing for something that math tells me will never happen, no matter the effort we make."

"Every child ever found had the same bad odds that Chloe and Huck do. We just have to believe. We have to take all the good energy in the universe and point it at where they are." Her eyes looked like the swirls from Van Gogh's "Starry Night," and then that weird magic she was full of that could have garnered a cult following came pouring out all over me again. That potion she reeked of, full of torture and serenity, both, was seeping out into the air around us...that scent that had intoxicated me worse than the beers I'd drunk in the alley all night. She was doing it again. I still thought she'd messed up bad by not going to the cops immediately when she realized that she'd seen my Chloe, but in that moment, all I had for her in my heart was forgiveness. I wasn't ready to tell her just yet. I wasn't that strong and had too much pride to carry.

"Knock, knock." The nurse pecked on the door.

"Come in." I sighed.

"The detectives are here to talk with you, Mr. Cianciola." She tried to sound upbeat as the two suits followed her into the room.

"I'll leave you all to it, then." Teal said quietly, eyes darting around at the specks on the floor tile.

"Thank you, Ms. McHone." One the detectives nodded toward her, obviously having met her already.

"We're, um, headin' back up to Folly tonight. We're gonna stay with my mama's Aunt Nadine until we can figure out a new place to live. Our house is now part of the investigation, I guess...and well, it was a Limeberry property, so, you know." She paused and shrugged her shoulders. "They said there's nothin' more we can do in Surfside Beach right now. Plus we can't afford anywhere to stay. I—um—I guess I'll see you around?" She said this like it was a question, then paused at the door and waited for me to give her something more than what I was able to in that small moment.

"Yeah. I'll see you around," I answered and turned my head away.

PART 4

TEAL

CHAPTER 26

The first 48 hours back in Folly Beach were the worst hours of my life. They were worse than when I first heard that Huck was missing. In that first stage of grief, the denial gifted a certain amount of hope; and the shock, a certain life-giving adrenaline. But once I got back to Folly without Huck and without our almost-house that, regardless of the shambles, was still my home, it was all just *real,* the new normal that chilled me to the bone. It was the first few glimpses of what a new life without Huck in it might look like…and *feel* like. I was experiencing the beginnings of a new era, a dark era that felt cold on a hot day. They were empty hours that passed me by, with no meaning, no home, and no more of that initial mania-fueled hope I'd sold so hard to Will back at the hospital. Everything had gone still, and I was alive in a void, a black hole that refused to spit me back into the space I was used to.

The search in Surfside was still going on, but it was random at best, just shot after shot into the dark. The cops had no leads, no clues, no paper trails, no Karen and still no alleged storage unit holding "the boy." It was as if Limeberry had been a ghost before he even died. Everything was just vapor, with nothing to hold onto or follow after.

Mama's aunt, my late grandmother's sister, Nadine, took us in, but she didn't pretend to be happy about it. She was in her late sixties, was widowed, carried the weight of an average 11-year-old girl, and smoked more than any person I'd ever met. Her voice went well with her addiction and turned me off immediately when she rattled off her list of expectations to us when we moved in.

When we first got there, instead of throwing her puny arms around us and asking about Huck, she cautioned us sternly not to let any of the cats out of the door. Five seconds later the scent in the air told me those cats hadn't *ever* been out of that house before. Aunt Nadine picked one of them up as he nuzzled her liver-spotted leg. She showed him the affection I would have thought she might donate to her grieving family, but it wasn't the case. She kind of looked us up and down one more good time before she shuffled back to the den in her pink dollar store bedroom slippers and bobby socks. And besides a glimpse of her here and there, screaming at Pat Sajak or Alex Trebek, that's about all I saw of her. But I didn't mind that she was scarce; that was one of the only perks at Hotel de Nadine.

As for Mama, she mostly slept, and I mostly sat and watched her do it. She'd take the tiny white pill, the one the doctors had given her a short supply of after they checked us out at the ER the day Limeberry died. They'd help her to sleep, but they certainly didn't stop her from crying and babbling on while she did so. She'd toss and turn and occasionally scream out some kind of gibberish. I'd hear Huck's name and even Hank's. They were always mixed in with the sobbing, kicking and snot-slinging. It was hard to watch. But I had to wonder what my own sleep was like. I'd often wake up sweating and sore like I'd been in a fist fight. The covers and pillows would be partially wrapped around by body, getting even skinnier than it had always been, and then partially thrown into the cat-piss reeking floor. Maybe my sleep was no better than Mama's.

The doctors had given me a bottle of the pills, too, but I didn't take them, even though they told me that I should. They'd said that it was just to settle me down a little bit, but I didn't want to settle down. I wanted to feel the pain. As long as I felt it, it would keep me motivated to find him. I wanted to be alert at all times even if it didn't feel good. I knew that it wasn't likely I would just stumble across Huck on the street somewhere, but I could pressure the police, demand they keep looking, and wrack my brain to the ends of the Earth. I couldn't risk taking something to dull me down when I needed all the sharpness I had. Plus, Huck deserved to have someone caring about him that much, hoping that much and willing him home with a clear mind. If I tried to ease my pain it would also ease my energy. And wherever Huck was, I knew that he needed me to send him all of the energy in my body. Our mother had none left to give either one of us anymore, and God bless her, she'd never had all that much to begin with.

I felt kind of sorry for her, watching her there while I picked at the tattered quilt that she slept underneath. It had claw marks at the edges and a variety of colors of cat hair all over it, almost a part of the design. And I couldn't help but wonder if that was where she might spend the rest of her life. I wasn't really even mad at her or resentful toward her anymore. I realized that maybe she'd been born with a smaller tank to fill, and that she just didn't have the capacity to give more than she had. Now, though, I feared the tank was gone all together, nothing left to pour anything good into. I worried that even if Huck was found somehow, that it would have all been just too much for her. There had been her own bad upbringing, whatever had happened to mine and Huck's fathers, the slew of men in between, the death of Hank Feller and now this. Huck's abduction. I knew that life with her was liable to become like living with a soldier returning home again from a tour in a warzone. I had to face the fact that whatever climbed out of her was likely not to climb back in all the way. I pictured her wasting away, skinnier than she already was, eating pills for breakfast and screaming at "The Price is Right" from the ugly green chair next to Aunt Nadine's. But who was I kidding? "The Price is Right" came on late-morning. She'd have to stick to Pat Sajak too. She'd never be up in time to banter with Drew Carey.

"I love you, Mama." I whispered to her and kissed her on the head.

She stirred just a little, her hair matted to the side of her face. It had aged years in a matter of days. Then she halfway opened her eyes and slurred something to me that sounded like, "Don't forget the milk."

I couldn't stomach the thought of it all anymore, so I did something I hadn't done in a while. I went outside and hopped on the rusty yellow bicycle that was propped up underneath Aunt Nadine's failing carport and cruised down to the oceanfront.

I parked the bike up against one of the columns

underneath the pier. The tide was at its lowest point of the day, which usually would have felt like walking into a gold mine for me. But it didn't. It felt lonely. Summer was over everywhere except for the calendar. School had started again, and everyone had gone home to the mountains or foothills they'd come from. The breeze was still warm but carried a scent that warned those left behind that fall would show up with its long list of responsibilities soon enough. I never realized until just then that the strange interim season had always been my least favorite. The party was officially over, seasonal businesses boarding up and battening down...no life left for me to watch from the nosebleed section. And that time of year, without Huck in tow, I really was alone. It was true solitude for the first time ever. I only thought I'd been lonely before.

I walked across a little river of water and up onto one of the sandbars that was only available to me at the lowest of low tides. I pulled a small metal shovel and a sifter out of my backpack, just in case something good happened to wash up, but I wasn't that enthused. I could feel the shadow of the pier beating down on my back, and it was cold...not on my skin, but somewhere in my soul. The last time I stood on that creaking wood, I'd been with Will, scared and suspicious of him, but connecting with him in that cosmic way that we did for the very first time. It felt somewhat sacred because of that. I feared that I'd never see him again, and that he would just live in this little compartment of my life that had been both magic and terror for a moment one summer. And I couldn't bear to think about it for more than that one second.

I tried, instead, to focus on the task at hand. I bent down and began running my hands over a shell bed, scraping a few layers off the top of it. Most people would just look right there at the surface, and that's why they'd never find anything either. But I knew you had to dig a little to get to the good stuff. I tried to hone in only on that and not on my loneliness for the two people that had left a big aching dry socket in my life. But I couldn't do it. I kept sucking air into the hole.

I hated myself the most for missing Will. I felt like I should miss Huck so much that I wouldn't have room to miss anybody else on top of it. But it turned out I had more room for missing people than I thought I did. And I also knew that Huck wasn't the only reason I didn't want to miss him. I'd been pushing it out of my head with all of the ado, but the fact was, I knew Will had slept with my mother. My *mother*. A cold shiver ran down my spine and almost triggered my gag reflex on the way. It made me as sick as anything could make a person. It did. I literally vomited when I woke up that evening and saw their shadows dancing when I went outside to look for my mother. Then I got nauseated again when she came stumbling home all disheveled and reeking of him. But what made me sickest still, and what I'd never say out loud, was that it didn't matter to me. I loved him anyway. Whatever his reason was for doing it—being angry with me, drunk, sad—I didn't know. But I knew it wasn't because their souls matched. The whole reason he hadn't gone all the way with me was because ours did. And that was all that I needed. Maybe it was the worst showing of self-respect in the world. Maybe it even made me a little pathetic. I knew it made me a traitor to every screwed-over girl on the planet too. But I didn't care. I loved him to the depths of the ocean and back. I couldn't help it. I. Could. Not. Help. It.

I almost let myself cry over it right there, wading in that tidal pool, and probably would have if I hadn't seen something dark in the sand after I'd gotten about four good layers down. I'd almost dug so far I'd hit water, and there it was, staring up at me, knowing what a proud prize it was.

"Oh wow. Talk about a needle in a haystack," I whispered to myself, unable to blink.

I cleared the area around the matte black mass, and carefully unearthed it to reveal its entire size. I then pulled a tape measure out of my bag and stretched it out beside what could only have been a

Great White tooth. It didn't look the size nor the age to have been megalodon. Plus those were usually hiding further inland, in the river beds where the ocean used to be.

"Just over two and a quarter inches long, and perfect symmetry. Dear God." I cupped my hands over my mouth. "Jackpot." I eyed the shark's tooth that came close to record-breaking size.

I carefully wrapped it up and stuck it into my bag, trying not to think about all of the things I could make of it, or of the money it could bring in as a single jewel-encrusted pendant. I'd found something truly amazing, one of a kind.

"Take that, Limeberry." I said out loud, remembering when he'd bragged about his private beach of treasures near Hilton Head Island, the one he'd so arrogantly bribed me with access to if I'd take good care of Will. All he'd cared about was keeping a good contractor. He'd had the man's daughter *kidnapped* for heaven's sake.

When I thought of it my stomach lurched and turned, and at first I didn't even realize why. I just felt nauseous and bothered in that distant way that takes a minute to make it all the way to your brain. But as I high-stepped through the sand back to where my bike sat against the tower of barnacles, it hit me, and it hit me hard. I might as well have stepped in front of a bus and let it mow me down. Limeberry's private beach. He'd said it had nothing on it, which was why it was so good for shell hunting…nothing but a little shed he'd built himself…a *storehouse*.

CHAPTER 27

I pedaled as fast as my legs could carry me back to Aunt Nadine's house. I'd somehow remembered to grab my prized shark's tooth before I took off, but I'm surprised at that, because I was consumed up to the neck in getting back as fast as I could. I imagined my wiry limbs flailing wildly from the rickety old bicycle as I pulled out in front of cars and blowing horns, but I really didn't know if that was how it went down. My eyes only saw my goal, and nothing else entered my mind. I don't even remember getting back, only that I'd recognized the yard, and jumped off the bike with the wheels still moving when I saw it.

I burst through the front door, "Mama! Mama! Get up, now!" I beelined for my cell phone that I'd left on the laminate kitchen counter next to the molding Wonder Bread. I called the direct number that one of the FBI detectives had left for me back in Surfside Beach.

"Special Agent Wrought." The voice answered immediately.

"Yes," I almost screamed. "This is Teal McHone. I'm Huck McHone's sister."

My mother cut in, still in a half stupor. "What in the world is goin' on? You kn-know where Huckie is?" She stumbled a bit, smiling kind of sick-like, as if she'd just been in the dentist's chair.

I waved her off. I wasn't trying to be rude, but I also didn't have the time to waste dealing with her. "I think I know where my brother might be."

"Tell me everything," Agent Wrought replied hurriedly, but calmly.

"It's just a theory, but at one point Mr. Limeberry had muttered on to me about some private beach he had on Hilton Head Island. He said that there was nothing on it except for an old storehouse he'd put up. I'd forgotten about it until somethin' jogged my memory today. I was thinkin' that maybe no one checked there because they were lookin' for commercial storage units or Limeberry-owned properties with known structures on them. This one could very well be undocumented. My guess is that nobody even realized it was there. It seems like that place was more of a private hideaway from the way he talked about it."

"I know the property you're speaking about," I was surprised to hear Agent Wrought say. "Our unit hasn't personally searched that one, but I know that it was in the Folly Beach file. Let me pull it up." I could hear things shifting about during several moments of silence.

"Teal, what are they sayin'? Tell me, sugar. Is Huckie comin' home?" My mother prodded, only slightly more articulate than she was before, her faded Guns N' Roses t-shirt barely reaching her thighs. She still leaned over a bar stool to balance herself on legs that looked a lot like the ones I saw on a newborn calf once when I was a kid.

"Just a second, and I'll tell you everythin', Mama. He's lookin' for a file to check on somethin'." I whispered, my hand over the receiver.

"Okay." Agent Wrought sighed. "I have a report here showing that the property was searched and cleared during the initial Chloe Cianciola investigation."

"That's really weird." I felt my upper lip curl up all confused. "Why was it searched then if Limeberry wasn't even a suspect at that time?"

"Maybe because Will Cianciola and Hank Feller both *were* when Chloe disappeared, and had worked at many Limeberry locations. But, like I said, it was cleared."

"For Chloe, not for Huck though. No one has

searched that property since Huck went missin', right?"

"That's correct. But the report states that there are no structures of any kind on that property. There is no mention of any type of storage shed. It actually explicitly states that the beach and surrounding lands are vacant."

"But that just doesn't make any sense." I scrunched up my brow. "Limeberry said to me that there was nothing there but good beach finds and an old storehouse. It was in a casual conversation. He would have had no reason to make that up."

"There's no mention of that structure here, but we can certainly check it out. It is possible that he lied for some reason."

"But that doesn't make any sense. Why would he make up the fact that he built a storehouse? That would be stupid. I actually don't think he even meant to tell me about it to begin with; it just came out in passin'."

"I don't know, Ms. McHone, but I can certainly send someone to give it another look for you. I promised we'd leave no stone left unturned."

"Who searched the property to begin with?" My wheels went on without him. "Who signed the report?" I asked, my eyes searching the space around me for answers, my mother still searching *me* for them.

"Um…it looks like an Officer Russell D. Smathers signed off on this one." He read it like a teleprompter.

"Officer Smathers?" The air ran from my lungs while they tried to chase it.

"Yeah. You know him?"

"Of course, I know him. He was the main officer working the Cianciola case. He went to high school with my mother. He *drove* me to Surfside Beach when Huck went missin'."

"Okay. Well, I haven't met him, but I'll tell you something bizarre. He is a Folly Beach cop. The Hilton Head police or a federal agent with unlimited jurisdiction should have been present for the search of that property. However, his name is the only one that I see here." I could hear him flipping through pages. "Was he close with Limeberry, by chance? Did you ever see the two of them together?"

"They were thick as thieves!" I screamed. "Everyone in town knows that. Do you think Smathers could have purposefully cleared that location so no one would look there, just hopin' it would get lost in a pile of paperwork somewhere? Could he be in on this too!?" Flashes of his warnings trying to point me toward Will or Hank Feller skipped through my mind. Had he been trying to *frame* them? He'd gone to every length in the world to steer me toward believing that one of them was the culprit.

"Teal, I'm gonna get some units on this immediately. We will notify you and your mother if we find something. Do not tell a soul, not a police officer, no one, period, about this, okay? Right now, you cannot trust anybody in Folly Beach."

"Yeah...okay." I answered. "But I'm not waitin' around here. Mama and I are comin' down to Hilton Head right now."

"I cannot let you do that. It could be very dangerous. These rings run deep, and for all I know, you could have a tail on you right now. It doesn't look good that someone you say you knew so well is popping up on the radar. You don't know how this might go. It could be nothing, or it could end in a shootout. Your being there could blow our covers or put your entire family in danger. If someone thinks we're wise to them, they could very well do something to Huck, then run."

"You think someone could be watchin' me!?" My heart no longer felt safe inside of my chest and started planning its own escape.

"It is highly likely. Your boss, and now possibly an officer of the law, whom you thought you could trust, are up to their waists in this thing. You don't know how far it actually goes. You and your mother have already been betrayed by people you've known your entire lives. I'm going to send some unmarked security your way. You and your mother are staying at your aunt's home, correct? The residence of a Nadine Smith. Is that right?"

"Yes, that's right." I huffed, a little bit annoyed and a whole lot scared.

"All right. Stay put. We'll keep you posted."

"So we're supposed to just sit here and bite our nails and wait?" I asked, now about to cry.

"I'm afraid that's all you can do right now. You can wait, and you can pray for a miracle."

CHAPTER 28

Sirens flashed about wildly from all of the squad cars, lighting up the night sky outside of the Medical University of South Carolina like the Charleston harbor on the fourth of July. I dashed out of the police escort vehicle that the feds had sent to pick up my mother, Aunt Nadine, and me. Mama was clear enough to get herself inside the building at this point, and honestly, I couldn't have cared less about Aunt Nadine. I think she might have lingered about in the parking lot, still in those ratty bedroom slippers, during all of the commotion.

I ran into the building, Mama trailing closely behind me. The officers tried to explain that when they found Huck in the storeroom that had indeed turned up on that Hilton Head lot, they had decided to have him transported by air to MUSC because of the much better facilities and proximity to our home.

But I heard very little of the facts they churned out at us. I only knew that they'd found him. The rest of it was trivial to me. Nothing else mattered in my whole world in the middle of that frenzy, not even Will.

Huck had been alone in that shed for over three days without any food or water. He was terrified, disoriented, and sitting in the dark in his own waste when they found him. But he was alive, and he was going to make it. The officer said he could barely speak and was in and out of consciousness when they picked him up off the concrete floor, but that he said one thing, *"I knew you'd come."* That got me the most. He hadn't lost faith in us when he was probably hours away from death, trapped in that hell. In the late summer, I was sure the heat had wrapped its arms around that place, making it an oven. I pictured him in there, sweating, starving, crying…and I could only be happy with one thing: I didn't give up either. Our faith merged together somewhere in the universe and rescued him. They found the Great White tooth on the beach, the needle in the haystack, and it was going to be okay.

When we got off the elevator that seemed to climb to the top of Mt. Everest before releasing us, the escorting officer handed my mother and me off to Special Agent Wrought. I remembered him when I saw him. He'd been in communication with

Detective No Name for the most part when we were up in Surfside. He didn't look like an FBI agent. He wasn't scary enough. He stood about 5'9", had a small frame and a white mustache. He wore a suit with no tie and his name badge around his neck on some sort of lanyard I might have made in middle school. He looked like a campus security guard, but no, he was the man who listened to my gut instinct and sent an entire fleet of officers to a tiny storehouse I'd heard about in passing. He saved my little brother's life.

"Ms. McHone," he spoke first to my mother, who still trailed me, taking us both by one hand each.

"Oh, thank you. Thank you," she sobbed over his attempts to speak. "I want to see him. Please take me to my son. I need to be with him now."

"And we're going to let you in just a minute. They've given him a lot of fluids, and he's coming back to us. Unfortunately we're going to have to question him as quickly as we can and get as much information as possible while it's fresh. We'll give you a few minutes with him first. But please do not ask him any questions or offer up any information about the investigation. We need untainted details from him. Do you understand?" He spoke kindly, but matter-of-factly.

"Yes, yes." My mother nodded wildly.

Then I asked, "Is he hurt? I mean other than the

trauma of being kidnapped and the malnourishment? Is he? Did anyone—"

"A parent has to be present for the full examination, but we have no reason to believe he was physically or sexually assaulted at this time. We can't say that officially until the conclusive exam is completed, but there are no initial signs of trauma unrelated to the heat or lack of food. He was found in the same clothes he was taken in. It appears that he was simply being held for transport, like a commodity, then neglected after Limeberry's death. Karen, of course, fled. We think the buyers got spooked when no one showed up to make the exchange. He was just left alone there. He is severely dehydrated and scared, but otherwise, all right. He wouldn't have been for much longer without you, though. Your brother owes you his life, Teal." The agent rattled the information off methodically, even the compliment. I wondered if he'd once been a soldier. I guessed a Marine.

"And Smathers?" I asked.

"In custody along with four other officers so far. But, there will probably be more arrests made. Smathers knows that policemen, and especially policemen who have hurt children, do not fare very well in prison. He's singing to us like a canary, which is a good thing. I'm confident we'll get to the bottom of this. It could take a little time. But we'll get there. I believe the entire ring could be shut down, or at least significantly reduced."

"Okay." I nodded along, my hands on my cheeks. "And what about Chloe Cianciola? Has she been located yet?"

Agent Wrought tried not to flinch, but his thin mustache twitched slightly. "There have been no other children recovered at this time. We believe they are already at secondary locations, most likely in another organization all together outside of the US at this point. We are working with international authorities, but the odds are not favorable for them at this time, I'm sorry to say. We've also been in communication with those families. You two are very fortunate to have Huck back and should consider his return a huge win for your family."

I finally let a tear escape its own hostage situation, and this time I'd let it out for Chloe, and maybe, also, for Will. I couldn't imagine his agony after the cops had taken his hope away.

"Would you two like to see Huck now?" the officer asked, with no other condolences offered.

We both nodded, grabbing the other's hands, no words waiting in either of our mouths.

"Okay, just remember. Nothing upsetting. Not a word about the case. Just hugs and love, all right?"

"Okay." My mother let a breath out and straightened herself up.

Still grasping hands, we walked past Agent Wrought and into the room where a much skinnier version of Huck with greasy, unwashed hair was hooked up to all kinds of tubes. But it was our Huck. I took in all of him immediately—the rogue freckle on his right cheek that didn't go with the others, his lack of earlobes, and the birthmark on his elbow resembling the crescent moon on the South Carolina state flag. It all rushed me like an early autumn wind on the beach front, stirring up memories and warmth all around my body, a sandy whirlwind that I was happy to be trapped in.

We ran to his bed like kids run for the sprinklers in June and threw our arms around him, his own skinny limbs struggling to get around the both of us at once. I could smell the unique scent of his skin, and could feel the tickle of his McHone curls as I tried to melt my heart right into him.

And no words were spoken. Instead, we all cried out of our identical sets of aqua eyes. The three of us embraced as the imperfect family that we were, battle-scarred but alive and together again. We cried there together; we cried out all of the pain and joy that an entire ocean could hold.

CHAPTER 29

I made my way to the waiting room after I got my few precious minutes with Huck. Mama had stayed back with him while they started his physical exam and questioning. I didn't want to leave him, even for a second, but I knew that now more than ever, I needed to step back for a moment to let her just be his mother. I'd see him again after his statement, which I knew would be hard. The cops would, as gently as possible, ask him a million questions about his captors and his time with them. By the time they'd walked him back through every smell, touch, taste, sight, and sound, and lead him on a brutal hike through his loneliness and his fear, it probably wouldn't feel so gentle after all. It would probably feel like climbing a rocky mountain with bare feet, but he was a tough little guy. And I knew he'd get through it just like he got through three lonely days in that dark storehouse. And then I'd be there for him.

I tried not to think about it as best as I could. I made my way to the snack machine in the corner of the room to distract myself with something that would aim to give me diabetes. Hospitals only offered the very best. The machine was one of those old-school kinds where you'd put the money in and wait for the spiral metal god to decide whether or not he'd release that Snickers bar you had been pining for. It was a toss-up how it would end. I would either calmly reach down and remove my candy, or I'd spend twenty minutes shaking and cussing at the shit contraption that just ate my quarters. At that moment, I didn't care either way it shook out. I could have just enjoyed the chocolate, or suited up for the fight. I'd have felt great no matter what after everything I'd been through.

"You've got to go for the Reese's Cup, not the Snickers bar. All the peanut butter will keep you going longer, you know." The voice from behind me was unmistakable. The way he'd said "Snickas bah" all Boston; it gave him away.

"Will?" I turned around slowly, shocked to see him there, even having heard his voice first. "What are you doin' up here? To be honest, I wasn't sure if I'd see you in Charleston again. I didn't know if I'd see you anywhere at all again."

"I had to come back to get my personal belongings out of the cottage...of course, after the cops had already rummaged through it all and left it in the mess from hell."

"I see." I nodded, rocking up onto my tiptoes and then back to my heels.

"One of the feds called and let me know that they'd gotten a good lead for Huck and would keep me posted with any updates. They told me when they found him. I can't imagine how excited you and your mom must be. I bet you two are over the moon right now." He smiled at me, truly happy, only an ounce of his own sadness in its shadow.

"Yeah..." I started slowly. "It's, um, it's really indescribable." I couldn't let myself smile back. I felt too much survivor's guilt. My story had a happy ending, where his did not.

"I hope I'm not imposing, being up here. I just felt like I needed to come. I don't know why." He shrugged. "Maybe to be close to someone's victory, or just to be a friend. I don't know. I said to you once before that everything is a little bit selfish. But, really, I am happy the cops found at least one of them."

"Will, they could still find her. They found Huck. Miracles happen. Every day." I tried, but was unsure if I even still believed it.

"They found Huck because Limeberry is dead,"

said Will, "and the operation fell apart before they could get him moved to the secondary location. Chloe had been gone for weeks already by the time they got your brother. They told me in the best way they could that she's probably out there somewhere, but that they couldn't begin to imagine where. I think I'd rather them have found her dead, to be honest. The thought of her just out in the world—" He choked up. "But, I'm never going to stop looking or trying. I'm realistic about the odds, but I will never give up on her. They gave me the name of a few agencies that can help and some support groups. All I can do is try and keep breathing while I do it. Someone once told me that breathing is sometimes the only goal, and that one day we'll know why, because it will all be worth something eventually. I'm going to try my best to believe that. I kind of think that I already have in some ways. When I was bleeding out that day, I knew that I didn't want to die. I guess that's a start, isn't it?" He shrugged with his hands in his pockets.

I reached out and threw my arms around him, and he slowly put his around me too. He accepted the affection that I tried my best to give to him, the small transfer of energy from my soul to his. I could feel him breathe in the scent of my hair and squeeze me just a little tighter for a moment before we finally let go of one another.

"I really need to get on the road now." He checked his phone then wiped his eyes. "But there is one more thing I have to say to you. I wasn't ready to when I saw you last. I was still so angry and cold toward you. But it needs to be said. It's the other reason I came up here—"

"What?" I looked into his eyes.

"I messed up. I was angry at you and mad at the world. Your mom and I, we—"

"I know." I nodded. "I could smell you on her when she came back that evenin'." I tried not to whisper and instead to sound assertive and direct, but I think I failed.

His face fell in shame. "I am so sorry, Teal. I was in a bad place. I'm still in a bad place. *Horrible,* but it's no excuse. I was just consumed by everything unclean in the world. I wanted some other impure, messed up, jaded body next to mine. So, I didn't fight it like I should have. It was nothing to either of us, I can promise you, but I know that it was probably something to you. And I'm sorry for it. For what it's worth, I will always be sorry. I'm fucked up, Teal. I can blame Jessica, or Limeberry, or Boston…it's probably all of it rolled up into a pill I swallowed that made me like this. You're too young and sweet, and pure, and good for me. I wanted to drink poison. I wasn't ready for the cure; I wanted more of the disease. That's why I did it."

"Did her soul look like yours?" I whispered again, but staring him dead in the eyes.

He put his head to mine, the tips of our noses just touching. "Not even close. I've only seen that once before. *Ever.*"

I began to cry for the hundredth time that day before I spoke again. "You said you had to get on the road. Where to?" I took my head off of his and looked into his eyes again, begging him to just stay with my gaze.

"I've got a cousin in West Virginia. Middle of nowhere. I think I'm going to go stay with him and hide out for a while, figure out what to do with myself."

"There's no ocean there," I warned, considering that the ultimate sin. The thought of living in a place without saltwater was as bad to me as living in a place with no air. I knew I'd just flop around on the dry land like a choking fish.

"I couldn't find what I was looking for on the coast. I couldn't up north or down south. I think I need some fresh mountain air. Pure, unsalted. I need a change, Teal." He shrugged.

"I know you've had a lot of bad stuff happen, but don't blame the ocean." I shook my head then added, "I'm sorry you didn't stumble across any beach finds worth hangin' on to."

"Don't do that, Teal. Don't take away the

connection we had by saying that. I did find something worth keeping, and I'll keep it forever." He paused. "I'll keep you with me forever."

"Then why leave me?" I sniffled.

"Because I will not steal your life. You're barely out of high school. You deserve more, and one day you'll see it. You're going to do great things and find love and happiness and all the things your heart desires. You'll remember me with a little hurt and a little happiness, and I'm glad you will. But you'll find something stronger than me to love too. I won't keep you from where you belong like a little caged hermit crab."

"But what if I want you to?" The tears kept flowing. "What if I want you to make a mess of me, so we can be that big amazin' mess together? Don't I have the right to want your mess?"

"I'm not going to let you. Because I love you too."

I shot him a confused look.

"I heard you say that you loved me before I passed out after I was shot. And I know you meant it. And I mean it back, so you deserve to hear it and to know it. But it isn't right the way it is now. You don't deserve to start out with broken love. Even if you don't see it. I've done it before and it doesn't work. If we're meant to be, one day when I have at least some part of my head back and you're old enough to be in love with, maybe we'll find each other again. But I can't do that to you now, not today. I need a change, and you need to be set free in the water where you should be. We'll never make it if we start from where we are now."

"You know, Folly Beach used to be called Coffin Island," I said. "It was good at gettin' rid of anyone that it didn't want to keep, but it seems like it won't let me go. I guess I'm just bound to it, like a lonely little mermaid that can only live in those particular waters." I shook my head.

"You are a mermaid." He smiled softly and continued, "but from what I know about them, they can grow fins or legs to their liking. A mermaid is meant for the ocean but is never trapped anywhere. You'll find your way, Teal McHone." He kissed me on the forehead before gazing into my eyes, and then brushing his lips light but lingering against mine.

And that was the last thing he said to me. He hugged me one more time, a long hug that was so tight it hurt. It was full of all of the things we didn't know how to say, full of everything that had happened that summer, and full of everything we wished it could have been instead. It was a hug that whispered to us about a future we might have had in another life, where time and age had been on our side. It was an embrace that we'd both hoped for a second would just carry us away to some other place, though we knew it could not. And finally it was a hug that said something our mouths didn't, a hard and cruel *goodbye*. Then he let me go, and I watched him walk away from the ocean.

CHAPTER 30

I stayed in Folly Beach for another two years after Will left. I still find it strange that I classify it that way, instead of *after I graduated high school*, or *after Huck was found*. But everything in my life had suddenly been divided into pre- and post-Will Cianciola. He was the river that flowed through all of it, separating my life into one side or the other of the steep banks he'd created around me.

I helped Mama with Huck while she waitressed at the little diner by the pier during the day and took virtual classes at Trident Technical College. This was during the Corona pandemic of 2020, so she needed all the help she could get. God knows, we all did that year, trying to work and stay healthy on top of everything else we were still reconciling.

She wasn't perfect and never would be, but after Huck came home, she stayed away from the booze, even during quarantine. But more importantly, she stayed away from men like Hank Feller. She still cussed like a sailor, and could burn an ice cube, but she tried her best to be a mother. She found her new calling as a dental hygienist, and got work at a small office just a few miles inland after life opened up again. We stayed at Aunt Nadine's cat emporium until Mama finished school, and right up until I left in the fall of 2021.

I started my apprenticeship with Casey Garvin about a month after Will left for his cousin's house in the mountains. I'd taken a solid four weeks eating tubs of Cherry Garcia and watching Judge Judy with one of Aunt Nadine's cats perched in my lap before I found my way back to digging up bones. Then Mama signed up for school. For once in her life she'd stepped up and led by example. She'd inspired me for the first time ever by putting away the pills and picking up a textbook. She traded that musty quilt she'd been sleeping under for a pair of scrubs and some dental floss, and I couldn't have been more proud of her. After an initial period of resisting from the hair-infested couch in my unwashed pajamas, I packed up the pity party too. She never said anything to me about it, nor did I say anything to her. But I think she knew how to be my mama this time. She let me grieve and then showed me the way out of it. She did something worth doing in front of me—

didn't judge me, or demand things from me—and it worked. She took care of me and Huck because she finally took care of herself.

I did my best to save every dime I made from working with Casey from the beginning. Even though I was motivated again, Folly Beach, itself, still seemed lonelier than ever. It was actually worse than just lonely. I'd even have called it spooky. It was my haunted house with reminders of the baggage that I'd recently found myself carrying coming from every cove and corner. A scent in the breeze, a red bucket lying in the sand, children running happily, the Limeberry Properties sign that still hung in the center of town…the ghosts had taken over completely.

It was barely October of 2021 when I finally got the chance I'd been waiting for…or maybe it was that I was finally brave enough to take it. With Mama done with school and moved into a brand new apartment with Huck, I really had no reason not to jump anymore. I'd put money back for two years and had no more reasons left to stay. I wasn't imprisoned by anything anymore. The Coffin Island warden had unlocked my cell, but for some reason I kept sitting in it, like some weird form of Stockholm Syndrome. But I knew, *I knew* it was finally time to stand up and walk out into the big, scary, wonderful freedom…the freedom that Will had wished on me the day he left.

It was the first cooler morning of the year when Casey came bebopping into our workshop in one of the little boho dresses she was famous for wearing. It was tied up and muddy on the edges, and she was sporting waders from where she'd been combing the Kiawah River ditches for product since dawn. I'd been sitting in safety goggles all morning, drilling holes for gems into bronzed megalodon teeth, when she walked in. I'd been working with her for two years, pinching every penny that I ever earned along the way, and it was time to let her know my plans. And hope she'd be happy for me.

"Casey." I took my goggles off slowly. "Can I talk to you about somethin' for just a minute, please?"

"Oh, you have your serious voice on today." She pulled her tan wide-brimmed hat off and sat it down beside me. "What's up?"

"I've been doing a lot of thinkin', and a lot of research lately..." I hesitated, feeling the weight of her murky eyes on me. "I need to get out of Folly Beach. I need to go somewhere completely different and start *my* life. I've helped my mother while she's been in school. And I think she can handle Huck on her own now. So, it's time. I need to walk away from all the chaos that's held me here and start somethin' new."

"Okay..." Casey nodded sympathetically. "Is this you giving me your notice? Are you planning on leaving soon?"

"Yes and no," I responded. "I have an idea, but I can't do it without your help."

"Okay..." She brought her hand to her chin and leaned back curiously into her wicker chair.

"You know that Huck was taken by human traffickers, and that I was heavily involved in the Chloe Cianciola case a couple of years ago."

"Uh huh." She tried to follow along, nodding slowly.

"Since then, I've felt the urge to do something about it, and I'm still not sure exactly what that might look like. But I have some ideas. I want to start a line of fine fossilized jewelry named Chloe Paige, after the Cianciola girl. I want to create a new division of Foxy Fossils, where some of the proceeds go to help the victims of human traffickin' in some way, whether it be rescue efforts, therapy for those who have been found or funds for task forces. I basically want to set up a non-profit organization funded partially by this new line. However, the line itself will also make more revenue for Foxy Fossils."

"So far, I love the sound of that, Teal," Casey said, looking as if she might tear up. "I'll need to see the numbers, of course. But you also said that you want to leave Folly Beach. So how will that work?"

"I've been researchin' fossil deposits around the world. I think I want the Chloe Paige collection to feature rare bones, teeth, and whatever else I can find from beaches around the world to represent the global impact of human traffickin'. Also, the more rare fossils will ultimately bring in more money. We'll *make* more, therefore we'll be able to *give* more, like to fund task forces and rehabilitation and stuff like that. I've been researchin' it a lot. I'd like to start out on the Jurassic coast of England in Dorset. It's like an open treasure chest for serious fossil hunters. I've saved enough money to get there and to live on for a few months while I get things up and goin'. However, I'll need help with equipment and marketin'. I need your brand awareness. So, I was hopin' that you might be ready to take Foxy Fossils to the next level...on a mission with me."

Casey sat back and looked at me for a second before she spoke. "Teal...you...amaze me." She shook her head. "You are, by far, the most hardworking person I've ever had on my team. There isn't a doubt in my mind that you can make this work. As long as the numbers are right, I'm happy to go on this journey with you...honored. I hate the thought of not seeing you here in the workshop every day, but I also know that this is something that you really need to do. I know what this particular thing means to you. And I think it will help a ton of people who so badly need it. So I say yes, let's make it happen." She nodded with glassy eyes.

"You're sure you don't need some time to think about it?"

"No. It's you. If you say you'll do it, you'll do it. I'm in."

I let a long breath out. "You have no idea what that means to me. I've worked on a business plan for this and have even consulted finance professionals on it. I have it ready for you now. I've just been nervous to pull the trigger for some reason. I'll email it right over for you to take a look at. I'm just so happy that you're excited about this…that you *get* it." My heart pounded.

"I can't wait to see it, Teal," she said and stood up to hug me. "More than that, I can't wait to see what Teal McHone is going to do with that great big world. You've got a lot of grit in your bones, girl."

PART V

CHLOE
NOVEMBER, 2034

CHAPTER 31

I stepped up to the microphone, trembling like a pebble on the ground in the middle of an earthquake. It was one of the first times I had trembled from excitement instead of from cold, or hunger, or the all-too-often touch from a rough, calloused hand. It was a new feeling for me, and I think it was more good than bad, but I was still deciding. I'd yet to fully weigh out the enthusiasm versus the anxiety, but I hoped the latter was losing. I had trouble recognizing happiness, but I was learning to do it. I'd learned that the body reacted similarly to the bad and good—shaking, sweating, panting—so joy was sometimes hard to pinpoint, but I thought that this was it.

There may have been some times when I was little, that something was so thrilling that I couldn't help but shake, but if there had been, I'm not sure that I remember it. I remember shades of happiness, glimpses of good times…just not all the way. What I do remember, however, is shaking so hard that my bony knees bounced off of one another when Karen tied my hands behind my back once we got into that van on Folly Beach. The first night. One of my first memories. It came right after a montage of more pleasant things, my mother blowing on my knee to ease the pain of a scrape, my father walking me into the first day of kindergarten...red-headed Mrs. McFall's class, the cherry off my ice cream cone hitting the ground on a sunny day.

It still sent chills down my spine, though, the memory of all memories. I'd lost sight of my father, and it was getting darker by the second. I was crying, and she called me by my name.

"Chloe, Chloeee! It's ok. I know your Dad. We work together. Come with me, sweetie."

So I took her hand. It was only minutes before I discovered the lie, though my gut knew it right away.

"Why are we getting in your car?" I'd asked. "My Daddy is still on the beach."

She said nothing, and I began to get more nervous. We drove no time at all, and she handed me off to two men I'd never seen before who tried to coax me into the back of their white van also promising to know my father. When I wouldn't go, my hands and feet were tied in two seconds, and my mouth was taped over. And that was the beginning of everything.

Instinct is there with us from birth. It isn't something you have to grow into. But, also, how do you process that at six years old? Like happiness is now, danger was hard to recognize then. It was just groping through new feelings, pawing at darkness.

I remember trembling again when I was given to my new "parents," a couple from Ukraine who spoke little English and had lost their own small daughter to cancer only a year before. The place where I was being held was run by a stick thin woman with a pointy nose named Ms. Platt. I don't know where that was, but I hadn't been on a plane yet, so it couldn't have been that far.

I remember hearing her say, "Oh you'll love this new one that just came in. She looks just like the photo of your sweet little one."

The couple came in shortly, looked me over, mumbled to one another in another language, signed a few papers, and that was it. I was then on my first plane, a small one with no other people that shook the whole way over the ocean when it carried me to the other side of the world.

I suppose they were pleasant enough compared to the others, my "parents". They didn't speak any English to me, but they didn't hurt me. But when it didn't work out, it didn't matter that I never knew what they said. They didn't have to say anything. It was because I couldn't actually *become* Oleksandra. So, I was taken to another place, one full of children...and exchanged.

All I remember was a large woman who looked like a potato saying in some accent, "aww, look at that face. We have stuck gold, yes?"

That's when I was shipped to Monaco, hidden in a truck full of cattle for however long that drive across Europe took. It seemed like years, but was probably only a week at best. But when you eat, sleep, and defecate in a moving barn around the clock, time drags its heavy feet. The stink from that could very well still linger on me today. I'm known to scrub it off as if it does, and have to have someone monitor all my showers still, so I don't rub my skin into rag-burnt patches...another thing I'm working on.

I remember that particular journey best of any I took. I could see through the slats in the back of the truck as we arrived around dawn. The buildings there were bright yellow and sunny, and the water a deep turquoise, not like the murky gray ocean water I'd seen on the South Carolina coast. But, then, Monaco was different than anything I'd ever seen, period. It was full of rich and famous people, actors and royalty. Men with gold chains hanging around their necks held the hands of women with diamonds in their ears. It was also probably the cleanest city I'd ever seen. It was a postcard decorated with jewels, castles and Ferraris. It was also the beginning of the dark for me. I only thought that truck was the root of all evil; but it didn't hold a prayer to Monaco.

That tiny country, only larger in size than the Vatican, is where I was groomed, pampered, and ripened for a few years until it was time for my virginity to be auctioned to the highest bidder. I lived with three other girls my age for almost seven years. That part wasn't the worst, once I came to terms with the fact that I was *not ever* going home. We were fiercely educated, bathed and fed. We had etiquette lessons from beautiful women, and were taught to appear as flawless, intriguing, and most importantly, pure creatures. We even had brief periods of recreation, what I would imagine to be normalcy. We'd spend an hour or two in the courtyard, braiding each other's hair, and learning about where everyone came from. We'd play monopoly or watch American movies in French. The other girls became my siblings, and I would often forget the reason I was there, which had never been kept a secret. Quite the contrary, actually. Our reason for life was to become pleasing for our gracious, high-paying bidder.

At thirteen, I was promised to a 57-year-old Saudi oil executive for the evening. My destiny had come to fruition. But I don't care to recount that, other than to say I would have rather gone back to the cattle truck. After that one night, my purpose was done. I'd grown into the perfect flower, then been plucked, and used for someone else's amusement. After that, I withered and died. I'd fulfilled the goal my sisters and I had been preparing for all those years, and was sent away. I never saw Vanessa from Spain, Olga from Norway, or Sophia from Italy ever again, but I'll never forget their names.

After Monaco came the blurry years. I no longer had my virginity, and my value was very little compared to what it had once been. The grooming, education, nutrition, short breaks to breathe in the sea...it all stopped. I was given one thing regularly, some kind of burning poison that was pumped into the IV to keep me "manageable." It was somewhere in Romania, in a town whose name I can't pronounce even though I've heard it scoffed at many times. That's where I was when they rescued me. And that's where my life and my story really began. That might as well have been when I was born, and was certainly the reason I decided to share my story today at the 2034 *Turn the Paige on Trafficking* Annual Event.

I took a deep breath for courage and brushed my thick brown hair behind my shoulders before I spoke into the mic, "My name is Chloe Paige Cianciola, and I am a survivor of human trafficking." I paused and accepted the wild applause.

CHAPTER 32

In that one breath I took before speaking into the microphone, I remembered the time in between *then* and *now*. I remembered when I was first rescued, and then thought of where I was now standing in real time...on a stage dressed like a girl who'd been cared for, about to go off to some quality college and major in Communications or some typical thing like that. It was a little over two years, a mere collection of months put together on a string, like Christmas lights. But it was the longest journey of them all, that interim.

I can't remember the rescue itself. I was too groggy from the drugs. It had gotten worse, and "they" had been keeping us in different levels of twilight for a while. At first we could play cards, watch black and white TV, read outdated magazines or paint our nails in between "customers". We got decent showers and small doses of time outside. It was kind of like a minimum security prison at first, like the one on that Netflix show with the tall blonde girl. One of the overseers, maybe the curly-haired one named Florin, would stream it on his phone and let me watch it over his shoulder from time to time...before things changed. It was his favorite show, the only one he'd watch. It made sense now, looking back...he related to it, being the warden of women. But when everything changed, even that one small joy came to a screeching halt.

It was the tall girl from Germany, the one taller than all the men that got brave one day. She had a sidekick, some girl who never spoke named Ulla, and together, they caused the shift. They made a break for it on a particularly sunny day when the overseers got lax, soaking up the rare light. It was unseasonably warm for Eastern Europe, and it caused cracks to appear, cracks big enough for one tall girl and one mute in a holey t-shirt to slip through. Ulla made it all the way, but the tall girl was shot to death after she scaled the barbed wire. After that, there were handcuffs, and tubes and needles...and then just a big blur, like TV static...until it changed.

I woke up in a white room with the sun in my eyes. It smelled clean, and the sheets were soft. I knew I'd either died and gone to heaven, or that I was in a hospital. When I opened my eyes, no one was there. So I just stared at the ceiling. I didn't know why I was there, and somehow didn't have the capacity to wonder why. I wasn't afraid, or happy, or sad. I was just there, waiting, numb.

When the nurse came in and discovered me wide awake, a team of other people came in rushing all about, faking calmness. I think it was a couple cops, a couple doctors, a psychiatrist, and a representative of some sort from somewhere who introduced herself to me as my "advocate." They all took turns talking to me, though I didn't talk back. I wasn't sure why. I didn't know if I couldn't or didn't want to. I don't know how long it was before I spoke, but when I did, it was to ask for more chocolate pudding. They'd spoiled me with the pudding, and it somehow gave me my voice back.

It was a few days before they let me see my father, but still long before I'd started asking for tasty treats. He was afraid to hug me, but I could tell that he wanted to. Same with crying. His eyes were always welled up, but he wouldn't let any water out of them. When he'd go back in the hallway I'd hear him gasping for air and occasionally punching the walls. And though I hadn't wanted a hug at first, I started wanting to give one. So about a month into my rescue, around the same time I really started to believe I was finally free, I did it. I hugged my father.

After that it was a lot of treatment and a lot of talking to women with small voices in "safe spaces." Some of it hurt; some of it helped. Some of it made me vomit; some of it made me cry, and some of it, eventually, made me laugh. All of it made me face it, understand it, or at least try to...the thing that my life had been.

I learned that I had only one incurable disease, which was considered a triumph because they could control the outbreaks and make it virtually undetectable. I learned that I could still bear children, and that I was surprisingly smart for someone who'd received such a limited education. They credited that to the vigorous tutoring I received until I was 13 in Monaco. I also learned that I'd need a whole new set of teeth, vitamin IVs for the known future, and a lot more talking on fluffy couches under weighted blankets. I learned that the night terrors might never fully disappear, and that I'd probably be in some type of counseling forever. But the most important thing I learned, that still hasn't sunk in *all* the way was that I was young, not old. I felt like I'd lived a hundred years, but at the time of rescue, had only lived nineteen. I could still have a life, they told me. Mine hadn't actually been stolen. I'd been saved. It took almost the entire first year to consider that possibly being true. And though I didn't fully understand it, I did learn to talk about it, and to hope for it.

My favorite thing to do was talk, much to my own surprise. I was never allowed to very much, not in Monaco under the strict rules of my teachers, and never in the brothels after. I'd been conditioned to whisper if I had anything to say at all. But one day, toward the end of that first year, my therapist told me to shout out in anger at everyone who had hurt me, to tell them what they'd done and scream at the top of my lungs all I wished my life had been instead. Then she had me scream out all I still wanted it to be.

When I finally did it, I shouted out, "Everything. I want to have a job, and an apartment, and a slice of real pizza from New York City. I want to shop for the perfect pair of jeans. I want to go bowling. I. Want. *Everything!*"

And I realized the power of my voice. At that moment it became my most prized possession in the world, and I thought that maybe, just maybe, I could use it to get more than chocolate pudding.

CHAPTER 33

The memories were fading, and I knew it was time to speak. I now had to say what I'd come to the convention to say.

"I was trafficked across greater Europe for nearly thirteen years. I was kidnapped at six years old while with my father in a sleepy beach town on the coast of South Carolina. It is a town legendary for people disappearing, from soldiers to tribes of Native Americans. My father had just told me the legend of the lost Bohickets, whose ghosts would rise from the sea oats, on the very night that I went missing. And now, here I stand today, a girl thought to be a ghost, rising from that mist. Though my story is tragic, it is one of the happy endings. I was rescued almost two years ago, thanks to this incredible organization. It was one of the task forces funded by *Turn the Paige* that liberated the brothel I had been held in for over five years. I am alive, and I finally know I am free."

The crowd stood and applauded once more.

"A teenage girl with a knack for making jewelry found a rare shark's tooth on Folly Beach in 2019, while I was a missing person. That shark's tooth was later encrusted with rubies in honor of the month I went missing, and became the first piece of fine jewelry in the Chloe Paige collection, named for me. Chloe Paige is now a nationally recognized brand and donates a portion of all profits to the victims of human trafficking for therapy, rehabilitation, medical care, and much more. However, it was the auction of that rare shark's tooth found in the beginning that provided funding for this amazing non-profit organization that saved me. I want to start by saying thank you, because I was that rare shark's tooth in desperate need of rescue. Thank you to this organization and to its incredible founder, Ms. Teal McHone, for saving my life. Ms. McHone, could you please stand?"

The pretty, slight-framed woman in her early thirties, who sat on the first row stood humbly and smiled, her cheeks turning slightly pink. She sat about a dozen bodies down from my father, who was the first to stand and clap for her with tears streaming down his face. They then exchanged the most peculiar glance toward each other and took a deep breath in perfect unison before sitting back down again. From the stage, I wondered what that pregnant breath meant, but continued on with the speech I'd been unknowingly writing for fifteen years.

"Ms. McHone has dedicated her life to rescuing children and adults just like me across the globe. Not only has she raised funds, she has connected with victims, and personally participated with the task forces. She's sacrificed having a family of her own to travel the globe looking for other people's children. The story today is not about what I went through for all those years. Use your imaginations, and it's worse. You all know what the things are that I endured at such a young age. I'm not here to go over them all in detail, but instead to be a testament for survival. Because of the people in this room, who've given up their own comforts, I am here and not there. I was not only rescued from what I can only describe as hell on earth, but was also given the support, the medical attention, and the help I needed to come back to life. The simple kind act of being offered a chocolate pudding was one of my first turning points, and asking for an extra one was the first time I spoke after my trauma. It was the first time I used my voice to get something I wanted for myself. But now I am speaking all the time, and I chose to speak to you all here today because I'm the one who was given her voice back." The crowd wildly applauded, and I could feel the goosebumps hatching down my arms.

"There are thousands and thousands of girls and boys out there in both the dark corners of the world, and right underneath our noses. They still have tape over their mouths, and we have to continue to fight for them. I am one of many, and we cannot give up. I believe more than ever that more happy endings are out there. Let's fight for the broken, and always, *always* speak for the voiceless. Thank you, and keep up the good work." I blew a kiss to the crowd and left the podium with tears in my eyes. I'd planned to say more, but I was overwhelmed. I was full of pain, of course, but more of gratitude, and of blessings…feelings so strong that I didn't have to guess what they were. But most of all, I was filled with excitement. I'd been reunited with my father on a beautiful spring day after almost a decade and a half of captivity, and today would finally meet the woman responsible for it. And this time, I was already used to hugs.

CHAPTER 34

My father met me backstage. It still shocked me to see him, even though we'd been reunited for almost two years now. It surprised me that his hair was halfway gray and that his crow's feet had gotten so deep. It surprised me that he still sounded and smelled exactly the same, and that his hugs hadn't changed a bit, either. He was really the same person. He was still unmarried and working in construction, though he had his own company now. Honestly, he looked great for 50, but it was just strange to get used to. And what was strangest was the height. I suppose his hadn't changed, but now that I was a full-grown 5'7", I could look him in the eyes if I wore heels. When I was little, he'd always seem as big as an oak tree to me.

He embraced me tightly and kissed me on the head, "You did such an incredible job, sweet girl.

You are so very brave." He still spoke to me how he had back then.

A young girl with a headset on then tapped my shoulder gently. "Ms. Cianciola."

I turned to face her and gasped when I saw the woman standing next to her.

"This is Ms. McHone—".

"Oh, my God! Finally!" I shrieked, and burst into tears as I threw my arms around her without any hesitation. "Finally!" I wept.

She joined me with her own sobs of joy and embraced me with equal force.

"Thank you, thank you, thank you. I can't believe I am just meeting you now. I wanted it to be sooner." I croaked into her hair.

"I've wanted to meet you for fifteen years now," she whispered back to me. "I heard you'd been found about a month after your area was liberated. I was working in El Salvador at the time and couldn't get back right away. We were knee deep in a huge operation. And…I know how it is in the beginnin'…that you'd need time." She paused and searched my eyes for something. Joy and pain maybe? She tested out the doses of both I had wrestling inside of me before speaking again. "I'm just so happy that this convention has brought us together. You and my brother, Huck, are the reason that I started the organization."

"I didn't realize you had a brother, Ms. McHone." I smiled.

"Yes, he was taken just weeks after you were by the same people but was quickly found. He's actually studyin' at Clemson University now. He would have loved to have been here today. Oh, and please, just call me Teal…"

"That's amazing." I couldn't help but smile. "I'd like to go to college myself…I think. I'm finally believing I can *eventually*. I'm still catching up with the schooling that I missed to try to get to that point…and I also feel like I need more time before I'm comfortable living on my own. I still have trouble being alone, or being away from the people I feel safe with."

Teal nodded with a warm smile.

"But I'll get there. The therapy the organization has provided me with has been just unbelievable. I hated it at first, but now it's kind of my lifeline. I'm a different person than I was two years ago. I still have the dreams occasionally, and that's hard, but in the grand scheme, I'm okay." I felt my smile start to droop when I thought back. "I wouldn't even let my own father hug me for a month. I couldn't stand to be touched. I barely said a word. I never thought I'd be standing up talking to people like I just did. I never thought I would feel like I feel today, maybe the best I've felt of any day I've ever had."

Teal beamed from ear to ear. "I'm so grateful that you were willin' to do this. I wanted to say to you that what you went through meant somethin'. Hundreds have been returned to their families because of what your hardship inspired. I should be the one sayin' thank you. I might have given somethin'. But you, Chloe, you gave everythin'."

"You both did." My father said, prompting Ms. McHone to finally release me and look him over with her mouth hanging wide open again.

"Will," she spoke more hushed than in a whisper, and then a little bit louder. "It's...so good to see you."

PART VI

TEAL

CHAPTER 35

Will walked slowly toward me, wearing all of his emotions on his face that had weathered just perfectly, like fine leather. His expression told me he was both grateful and fearful. But I was a thousand things more tumbling one on top of another.

He paused for a second, as unsure as I was about how we should greet one another, but he then pulled me to him and embraced me tightly. "I owe you my entire life."

"You owe me nothin'," I said into his shoulder, breathing in every memory of him, his scent exactly the same.

"Yes, I do. Because you were right. It all turned out to be for something."

"It did, didn't it?" I patted at his suit as I pulled back. "I never saw you in anythin' like this. It looks good on you."

"It decorates an old man well, I guess."

I shook my head, then said quietly. "The years have been good to you. You look great."

"I was going to say the same to you," he replied. "You're even better, and I didn't think that was possible. God...Teal..." He shook his head. "I was hoping to see you here."

"I didn't realize you two knew one another," Chloe said, wiping the tears off of her own lightly freckled cheeks.

"We're old friends." I winked at him playfully, realizing I must have looked like a love-struck teenager with the tears and longing springing out of my eyes. But, damn, it was all still there...whatever it had once been a decade and half ago. It walked in with him, and stood right there with us.

"How did you never tell me that?" She looked at her father. "I mean, I knew my case meant a lot to her, but I thought it was just a cause. I didn't realize it was *personal.* How did you two meet? I'm sorry, Teal." She redirected her attention to me. "Did I meet you before? When I was a child? Sometimes my memory isn't great...I forget things...I—"

"No, not really." I forced a warm grin, though the image of her frightened face that night on the beach streaked through my mind, bare and screaming. "It's a long story."

"Well, I'd love to hear it," she said, darting her eyes between her father and me. "My father and I were going to get a bite at the restaurant on the roof of our hotel just downtown. It has a great view of the water. Would you like to join us? To celebrate, I guess? Isn't that what you do in these situations?" She fidgeted, and I realized that was probably the first dinner invitation she'd ever extended to anyone. Who would I be to reject it?

I opened my mouth to speak but then looked at Will, as if I couldn't make the simple decision without him. There was, of course, the obvious concern, that Chloe wasn't ready for such an outing so close to the place she was abducted, overlooking the same body of water. But there was something else, too, like maybe I wasn't ready for such an outing. Maybe I couldn't just sit down and dine with him like it was all so normal. Maybe he didn't want to sit and dine with me after all this time. And maybe it was oceans of other things I could never organize enough to say in the tiny pauses life gives us to respond within.

"I'd like that." He nodded while my mind rambled on. "I would really, really like that."

"Me too," I said, so simply, but confidently, somehow letting him know all the other things, feeling him read me like he had back then.

Then I looked at Chloe. I was still in such

disbelief that the three of us were at the same place at the same time. It was the strangest dream, like a wonder of the world I thought I'd never cast my eyes upon. It was something I'd put out there and believed in, but like I'd believed in folklore…the way I believe that a man really did walk on the moon, almost at a hundred percent, but not quite. There was always this awe and mystery around it all, that maybe it couldn't be real, that she wasn't real.

"I've been looking forward to eating at this place since we arrived," said Chloe. "I'd missed that smell…like fish and mud and wind. I think they call it pluff mud or something. It was a smell I've never forgotten. The best smell in the world. It's so strong blowing up Vendue Wharf. I can't wait to smell from the rooftop. I bet it's even stronger." She smiled and shut her eyes thinking about it, and I realized it had been part of the hope she'd held onto since the beginning.

"Are you sure about that?" Will asked, his face ready to protest. "That smell could trigger other memories for you too. You've come so far, but I don't want you to push yourself because you're on this incredible high tonight. You've had things in public upset you before that you didn't expect. You have nothing to prove. Teal and I both can see how very brave you are." My stomach bounced off my knees as he spoke. I thought of all she'd been through, and how good she was in spite of it. I'd been told how she was found, ribs showing, attached to a dirty IV drip, only a camisole on, unable to speak or be touched. She was a far cry from that in this moment.

"This won't upset me. I've never thought of that smell as being part of the nightmare; it was the last happy place I had. That last summer before I went missing was the best we'd ever had together, Dad. The little pieces of memories of it carried me through some of the worst times of the whole ordeal." She put her hand on her father's arm.

"I've come full circle," said Chloe. She shook her head emphatically, bravely. "I reemerged. So maybe I'm the breaker of that curse on Folly Beach. I'm not letting the bad in the world take the sea away from me too. Nobody owns the ocean, and I own the memories. The memories are mine, and the future is mine. The in-between of it all can go to hell. Folly Beach wasn't my coffin. Charleston won't bury me tonight either. The smell of the ocean in South Carolina doesn't haunt me; it was and is my *hope*."

"Okay. Then that's what we'll do." Will gazed at me again, nodding to Chloe's bravery, then lingering past it. He seemed unable to just glance at me and look away like he would a normal person. I liked it.

I smiled, lingering on his face the same way. "It's been a while for me too," I said. "I haven't been back here in forever, it seems. You're right, though. Nobody owns the ocean."

"And it's getting dark now too," said Chloe. "I like the ocean even better at night for some strange reason. It feels like the time when wishes can come true, and now I know that sometimes they do." Chloe looked at me with a slight closed-mouth smile that hinted at the face she'd worn at six years old.

Will laughed out loud when she said it…then shot me a knowing look, ready for one of my famous opinions about such a phenomenon. So I took the cue.

"Personally, Chloe, I think it's magic." I smiled at her, then directed my attention to Will. "It's the only place that I've ever gone to search for somethin' in the dark and have actually found it. Sometimes it takes a while, and I feel like I dig for forever. Sometimes I have to leave it and come back to it. Sometimes my fingernails end up broken and bloody by the time I get to the good stuff… but it'll always wash up when the timin' is just right, whatever *it* might be. I've found it there, waitin' on me…every single time."

DISCUSSION QUESTIONS

1. Do you think it is easier to connect to people who have been through the same bad things in life that you have? More than the good? Why did the characters choose to connect in this way?
2. What are your thoughts on the relationship between Teal and Will? Was Teal too young for her feelings? Did Will stop soon enough? Do gray areas exist?
3. What are your thoughts on Tracy McHone? Is she a villain, or is she a victim? Did she redeem herself?
4. How do you feel about Teal's decision to hold back information about Karen? Is she partially responsible for Chloe's fate?
5. What is the significance of Teal's aspiring profession? Why does she shell hunt, and

how does it hint at what's to come?
6. Discuss the suspects in the novel. Who did you imagine to be the perpetrator? Were you surprised?
7. What comments does the setting make about the ebb and flow of life, and times of happiness verses times of despair? Consider the changes of the elements. Are they meant to guide in a deeper way?
8. Should Will and Teal forgive each other for the things they've done to one another? Will the timing ever be right for them, or did their time already come and go?
9. Were you surprised to hear Chloe speak at the end? Why do you think the author chose to give her a voice?
10. What is the significance of the ending? What does the future hold for Will, Teal, and Chloe?

ACKNOWLEDGMENTS

I have many people to thank for making this book happen...God is first and foremost. Without his favor my dreams would just live in my head. My husband, Kimsey Hollifield is always my biggest fan, followed closely by my parents. Whenever I finish a project, I always think back to my roots. I come from a tiny Appalachian town where things are small, and people celebrate the simple joys in life. However, those people are the ones who encouraged me to make my dream BIGGER always. I had an amazing time growing up, with the best friends and family. Their belief in me has always mattered and I thank every one of them for it.

I'd also like to thank my editor, Nicole Seitz. Her attention to detail and amazing insight made the book what it is. She also has an incredibly talented daughter, who long before this book came to fruition, had made a painting destined to be the cover. Thank you for letting me have your incredible art to represent my story, Olivia Seitz. You have a big future ahead.

Finally, I'd like to thank all of the brave survivors of human trafficking. This story was about a lot of things, with the trafficking lingering in the background...because that's where it lingers in our society. It is always there while the rest of our lives keep spinning. Let us never forget them, and always keep fighting.